THE HIGH PRIESTESS

MAYA DANIELS

BOOKS

Vinci Books

vinci-books.com

Published by Vinci Books Ltd in 2026

1

Copyright © Maya Daniels 2020

The author has asserted their moral right to be identified as the author of this work in accordance with the Copyright, Designs and Patents Act 1988. This work is a work of fiction. Names, characters, places and incidents are the product of the author's imagination or are used fictitiously. Any resemblance to actual persons, living or dead, places and incidents is entirely coincidental.
All rights reserved. No part of this publication may be copied, reproduced, distributed, stored in any retrieval system, or transmitted in any form or by any means, including photocopying, recording, or other electronic or mechanical methods, nor used as a source for any form of machine learning including AI datasets, without the prior written permission of the publisher.
The publisher and the author have made every effort to obtain permissions for any third party material used in this book and to comply with copyright law. Any queries in this respect should be brought to the attention of the publisher and any omissions will be corrected in future editions.
A CIP catalogue record for this book is available from the British Library.
Paperback ISBN: 9781036705831
The EU GPSR authorised representative is Logos Europe, 9 rue Nicolas Poussion, 17000 La Rochelle, France contact@logoseurope.eu

By Maya Daniels

The Necronomicon Guardian
The Magician
The High Priestess

Chronicles of Forbidden Witchery Series
Resting Witch Face
Pitch a Witch
Witch Please
Payback is a Witch

The Broken Halos Series
The Devil is in the Details
Speak of the Devil
Encounter with the Devil
The Devil in Disguise
To Look the Devil in the Eye
Better The Devil You Know
Give a Devil His Due

The Last Note Series
Sound
Sonata

Hidden Portals Trilogy
Venus Trap

The First Secret

Daywalker Series
Investigated

Infiltrated

Instigated

Initiated

Infuriated

Ignited

Infernal Regions for the Unprepared
Black Hand

Lower World

Everlasting Fire

Place of Torment

Hellfire To Come

The Courtless Fae Series
Secret Origins

New Blood Rising
Rebirth - Risorgimento

Overthrown - Rovesciamento

Recognition - Riconoscimento

The Gatekeepers Legacy
Legacy of Water
Legacy of Fire
Legacy of Spirit

Honor Among Thieves
Stolen Magic
Stolen Oath

By Maya Daniels
The Cursed Kingdom

Prologue

It had been a week since my life took a turn for the worse, sending me in a downward spiral that would lead me on a path with no positive outcome at the end. Struggling with my powers and making sure I stayed alive in a house full of killers seemed like a walk in the park compared to being bonded to a book the supernatural world would kill to get their hands on. As you know by now, I was the unfortunate soul who got shackled to it the night I killed the one person I hated with the strength of a hundred burning suns. The slug killed my parents, so I killed him in return. Unfortunately Karma smacked me in the face and dealt me a new set of cards.

The Magician was gone, his body turning into a tarot card I kept because of a nagging feeling I might need it in the future. The bloodsucker who forced me to go and steal from the leader of the mage faction almost died himself in the fight, which left me confused as hell about why he even bothered coming to my aid in the first place. Making sure that the book ended up in his hands could've been what brought him barging in the room, but that still didn't explain why he was threating The Magician in an attempt to protect me.

Nothing made sense.

Coming to Tia's apartment and dragging Glenda with me might've been a bad idea too, but neither her nor I could go back home. My uncle took control of the Mage's guild, holding the position of the Magician, and with that making sure I couldn't go anywhere near him. If I did, he would know I was trying to hide something. I had never been good at lying, and without Tia's help there was no way I would've pulled off the biggest lie I'd ever told: Nigel Thatcher was dead. The fact that the bloodsucker was prancing under their noses and going by the name of Blade was a whole new bullcrap I didn't have energy left to decipher.

Tia and Glenda spent two days interrogating me about what had actually happened and what it all meant for us until I was so frustrated that I told them everything just so I could have a moment of peace. Now I couldn't step foot outside without them following me like a bad smell and calling themselves my sidekicks. I knew it was all Tia's fault, but there was nothing I could do about it. The picture of the High Priestess the Necronomicon showed me that my troubles were just beginning, and if I wanted to survive, I needed to make sure Nigel Thatcher was alive. He had more information about the Necronomicon than any other person I knew, and I needed to corner him to find out just how deep the rabbit hole went.

Speaking of rabbits, the glass statues of the long-eared buggers sprinkled around the hotel Nigel was using seemed very fitting. It was my next stop, if only I could find a way to escape the two women adamant on coming with me. It should be easy for an assassin to sneak out.

A normal assassin could pull it off for sure.

A clumsy one like me? Not so much.

Still, I had to try.

Wish me luck.

Chapter One

Granby street was buzzing with activity as I sulked in the shadows behind the same tree I used as cover in hopes of finding any information on Nigel Thatcher. That was the time in the past when I was naïve and I thought I had any chance of assassinating the elusive vampire. I totally expected that son of a cracked nut to give me an ulcer by the time I killed him. I didn't end up with that diagnosis, but I did get shackled to a more sinister pain in my tush. The whispers slithering through my mind sounded distant the further I was from the damn Necronomicon book, but they were there. A constant inside me, reminding me that my life has gone to neverland, and no wishing or yelping "oweee" would make it go away.

No, I was royally fudged.

The IRS parking lot was almost empty—as per usual at the time of the night—only tonight it was giving me unnecessary anxiety. I couldn't understand the reason, but I knew deep down that something was going to happen. Rubbing my sweaty palms off the fabric on my pants, I stared up at the puffs of gray clouds stretching like a beaded necklace above the Glass Light Hotel and Gallery. As I watched, they floated through the dark sky to hide the few stars sprinkled through it. I had an inkling that this was where Selena took Nigel, and I had every intention on talking to the bloodsucker tonight.

It was his fault I was in this mess.

My heart hammering against my ribs, I locked my gaze on the hotel's front doors and glared at them like all of this was somehow their doing. The rustling behind me stiffened my spine and I braced as if I was about to be attacked. But it wasn't an attacker. I'd recognize the energy slamming into my back anywhere, even if my eyes were closed.

"Let me tell you how the story goes." The whispered words were enthusiastic enough to make me grind my teeth. "This is a rollercoaster of a ride—"

"Tia, if you don't stop it, I swear I will zap you. Why are you here?" Hissing at her over my shoulder, I clenched my fists so I didn't grab her by the neck when she grinned at me like a fool.

"What do you mean, 'why am I here?'" Undeterred, she rushed to my side, her eyes wide with excitement. "Sidekick, hello! Where you go, I go. All the adventures of the hero need to be recorded by yours truly. You're welcome, by the way. I won't charge a penny for anything."

"I'm not sure she appreciates humor, or us being here," Glenda muttered under her breath, edging nearer while tugging on Tia's shirt to prevent her from coming closer to me. The seer knew me well enough to know not to get within arm's reach of me when I was angry. "I told you it was a bad idea."

"Yeah. She needs to work on her gratitude issues."

Somehow Tia managed to take their interference and turn it around to make me the bad guy in the situation.

The giddy twinkle in their eyes and the eagerness plastered all over their faces did not match the apologetic words they murmured as they crowded around me, but their nearness did give me a case of claustrophobia. To my horror, I also realized both were dressed in all black, their pants and long-sleeved shirts sticking tight to their bodies and paired with soft-soled boots to hide their footsteps. My gaze snapped from their feet to Glenda's face and she had the decency to look ashamed.

"I had to sneak back in the clan manor and get some of my things." The seer told the tips of her boots, her pale face darkening at her cheekbones. "You left, and to stop Tia from following you, I asked her to come with me. Not that it worked, but yeah. She waited, hidden across the street." Glenda rushed to assure me when I sucked in a sharp breath. "I figured no one would care that a few pair of boots went missing. What, with everything going on, they could've gotten misplaced ... or something."

"I must've done something horrible in my past lives to be punished like this." Groaning, I turned my back on both of them and rubbed a hand harshly over my face in frustration. "This is Karma in the works right here." Taking a deep breath and blowing it out slowly, I scanned the front of the hotel across the street, seeing nothing. "At least you blend in with the shadows and no one will see you here, since this is where you will stay so I don't kill you both. There is that."

"Oh, look." Whisper-yelling, Tia ignored my threat and yanked on my arm to make me look at what she was trying to show me. "I made sure we have our signature added to the outfits, too." Puffing out her chest, she pointed a finger at her left boob.

I blinked stupidly, not understanding.

This night was going to smithereens really fast and I'd only been stalking the hotel for a couple of hours. My friends were adding to the disaster, and not just because they followed me here, but also because they were talking in riddles, which was making a heartbeat pound in my temples. The confusion I felt was obvious to both women, who held their breath while they waited on my reaction. Tia looked down and her eyes widened as if something clicked, then she stepped out of the thick shadow cast by the tree until the yellow glow of the streetlight fell on her chest. My stomach dropped and the base of my skull went numb when I finally saw what she'd been trying to reveal. Right there, on top of her left boob in elaborate swirls, were my clan's emblem, two dragons twining together, and my initials. Darting my gaze to Glenda's chest, I saw it on her shirt, as well.

A jolt of magic coursed through me until my fingers twitched and tingled.

Fear ... shock ... I had no idea what it was, but it was trying to strangle me.

"I made it the exact shade of blue." Oblivious to my turmoil while I wrestled with my magic and did everything possible for my swords not to appear in my hands, Tia kept jabbering on. "It matches the color of your eyes," she informed me proudly, while Glenda nodded in encouragement from behind her. They had a death wish, both of them. "When you do your thing, only your eyes can be seen with that face covering you wear. It's a perfect signature, I'm telling you."

The High Priestess

"Umm, Tia?" The timid way Glenda's voice filled the silence matched the way she inched away from me when her eyes zeroed in on my fingers, which were spasming as I fought the urge to release my power. Of course, the human ignored all signs of danger. Typical Tia, if you knew the girl. "I think we should go ... like now."

"Don't be absurd." Jerking her arm out of Glenda's grip, Tia stepped closer to me and a grin stretched her face. I realized in disbelief that she had makeup on, and a tiny dragon painted with eyeliner on the top of her cheekbone. It looked like a beauty mark when she was further away from me, but now it was mocking me. And all I could do was gape at it.

My mouth worked soundlessly.

"Sooo, are we going in to get intel or what? We can spread out, that way we can do it faster. It's what they do in all the spy movies I've watched ... I think." Tia muttered the last part under her breath, though her words still sent my eyebrows to my hairline. "I could get a nun to confess her sins if I put my mind to it. We will find the hottie in no time ... well, as long as I corner one of the hotel workers." Latching onto my forearm, she shook me in her excitement. "What do you think I should go for? Bad cop or good cop? I think bad cop will work the best, especially if they hear you swear. No way you can pull off bad cop. No offense Charlie."

I could hear her voice coming from far away, the sound echoing as if it was coming from underwater. A red haze blanketed my vision, one specific remark throbbing in repeat through my head. *"She'll find the hottie."* My internal voice mocked me, even adding sinister chuckles to drive the point home. The light coming from the street reflected off the glittery substance Tia used to draw the dragons and my initials on her shirt. Another joke on my account, and it laughed at me in the face. Somewhere deep down I was aware this behavior was unlike me and had everything to do with my connection to the cursed book, but I was too gone to stop what was about to happen. My rational brain screamed in panic because my friend was standing too close to me. Unfortunately, I was beyond the point of no return.

Everything happened too fast to track.

My fingers snapped open and stretched wide. The weight and the cool feel of metal instantly settled in my palms when both swords shot out. On their own, my arms moved, the muscle memory guiding my actions and slashing the air in an upward arch. My heart stopped when a flash of red passed in a blur before my eyes, and Tia's yelp followed right behind it. That was Tia's blood spraying from a wound I had caused, and I knew it from the bottom of my heart.

The horror didn't end there. My other hand cocked in preparation to remove the object of my anger at all costs. No struggling could gain me the control I so desperately wanted. Grunts and groans bounced off the pavement, the noises finally snapping me out of my daze in time to change the trajectory of my sword. I wished the returning logic had flicked my hand outward, but it didn't. No, it twisted the blade inward and the sword glided into my own thigh like it was slipping through butter. My mouth snapped shut, and my teeth clenched so hard I thought I broke a molar.

"The fuck is the matter with you?" Tia's anger was a tangible thing curling around my ears, and the best sound I had heard in my life.

I didn't kill her.

The High Priestess

My knees buckled more from that knowledge than the excruciating pain in my leg. Blinking fast to clear my vision, I looked down to find them both—her and Glenda—sprawled on the ground at my feet. Two pairs of glaring eyes were focused on my face, but I couldn't care less. A blur of red tackled Tia away from my weapon, and I realized soon after seeing it that it was Glenda's hair. If I wasn't so happy none of them were hurt I would've wondered how she managed to be so fast. That thought evaporated when another wave of searing pain passed through the muscle of my thigh, which reminded me I still had a magical sword sticking from it.

"Oh my God, you stabbed yourself." Tia, ever the observant, forgot about her anger as she scrambled on the ground and lifted to her knees, blinking in amazement at my bleeding leg. "Who does that?"

Embarrassment hit me out of nowhere, that question bringing old insecurities about being an Assassin Mage to the forefront of my mind. A lump formed in my throat. Attempting to play it off as nothing more than a scratch, I grinded my teeth to stop myself from crying out in pain when I reached for the trunk of the tree to lean on it.

"It's nothing." A squeak ripped from my throat when my hand missed the tree and I went toppling to the side.

My gaze locked on Glenda's, her owlish stare adding to my spiked heartrate a second before I hit the ground. The sword jostled in my leg and sent a fresh wave of agony through me, which only added to the pain from the impact my whole left side took when it kissed the unforgiving concrete. My head bouncing off the pavement, I rolled on my back and waited for the burst of stars behind my eyelids to go away. When my vision cleared and the agony had subsided, I didn't want to open my eyes. I could feel the heat from the bodies on both sides of me. When they didn't go away after a few minutes, an oppressive silence tugged on my neck like an anvil until I blinked. I had no choice then, so I focused on the two faces leaning over my head.

"Oweeee."

My whisper-yell made Glenda's lips twitch at the corners, though she flinched while at the same time. At least I thought it was because of that, but then Tia yanked the sword from my leg and I bit my tongue so hard I tasted blood.

"There." The clinking of metal bouncing off the ground faded with the rushing of blood in my ears. "She should heal on her own now, right? I didn't just kill her?" Tia's eyes were on Glenda for confirmation, while I debated on taking the sword and this time really stabbing her in the eye.

"Yeah." The seer nodded, her eyes never leaving me. It was almost as if she was reading my mind and expecting me to do what I was thinking. "She'll heal, but I'd stay away from her if I were you, at least for a while."

"Whatever. This is why she needs a side kick. I'm hoping bleeding in a parking lot will bring that point home." Tia huffed, and I turned to her because I was astonished that she really didn't give a damn about her life. "It's Charlie. She wouldn't hurt a fly, little less me. Have you met the girl?" When Glenda's gaping expression matched my own, the human chuckled. "Now ... when are we getting inside the hotel?"

"It's going to be a long night." I groaned as I stared at the sky and rethought my life choices, though it was difficult not to scream as my skin knitted back together and wave after excruciating wave of never ending pain crashed through me.

"Yup," Glenda chirped, and then she stiffened and peered over her shoulder at the entrance of the hotel, adding to my misery with her next words. "And if that's who I think it is, things just got much, much more interesting."

Chapter Two

"What is that dimwit doing here?" Wincing from the tightness of my freshly healed skin when I lifted on my knees, I glared at the person exiting a black vehicle parked at the front of the hotel.

"Who are we talking about?" Tia wiggled between Glenda and me, squinting to see what we were looking at.

"Jonas," Glenda spat the name in disgust, reflecting my sentiment when it came to that particular mage.

"The first target was spotted and is about to be eliminated," Tia whispered in a rush as she bent her head to her chest.

Reluctantly pulling my gaze from Jonas just as he disappeared through the front doors into the belly of the hotel, I incredulously turned it on my friend. "What are you doing?"

"Nothing." Her head jerked up and she shoved her left hand behind her back. Glenda's pained groan did not help matters either.

"Tia."

The High Priestess

Hissing her name as a warning, I stared her down until she huffed a breath and dropped her shoulders in defeat. Sluggishly she brought her arm around in front of her and uncurled her fingers from a black device that resembled a remote control. No, not a remote control.

A mother-trucking recording device.

"Hey!" she yelped when I snatched it from her hand and clawed at the air in a futile attempt to get it back.

Holding it away from her, I battled with my frustration while sending a wave of magic through my hand into the device to destroy it. Better it than zapping my friend for this stupidity. Sparks burst from it, frying it and blistering my own skin in the process. My teeth clenched, and I swallowed the scream that tried to push through my lips. Just because I ended up bound to the Necronomicon didn't mean I had miraculously gained control over my powers. They still worked more against me than for me, as demonstrated with the recorder.

"The two of you need to go home, now." Sounding pained—because I was in pain with my newly blistered palm—I shook my hand to drop the now melted plastic. "I can't do this if I have to worry about you, too."

"I just didn't want to forget any details," Tia grumbled, pouting like a petulant child while looking at the lump of plastic next to my leg. "You didn't have to destroy it. All you had to do was tell me to put it away."

I stared at her.

"Come on." Glenda, never the one to handle drama well, tugged on Tia's arm. "Let's go guard the book while she does her thing. She will tell us when she needs our help." Giving me a pointed look, the seer jumped to her feet. "Right, Charlie?"

After a long stare down I said what was expected. "Right."

Anxiety was eating a hole in my stomach. I wanted to barge inside the hotel and find Nigel. Also, I desperately wanted to know what Jonas was doing here. And I needed these two brickheads to go home where they would be safe. My thoughts must've been clear on my face because Tia didn't argue, although she glared at me while Glenda dragged her away. I waited until they disappeared into the darkness of the parking lot before bringing my hand to my chest and cradling it.

"Oweee." I blew on the blisters, although I knew it won't help. And as I expected it didn't do much, not until they start healing anyway.

The wind whistled through the branches swaying above my head, the occasional horn and roaring of vehicles accompanying it in a distant melody penetrating the rushing of blood in my ears. Melted plastic smarted like the dickens on bare skin, but I'd go to my grave before I admitted it to anyone. Left alone with no witnesses, I permitted one tear to trickle down my cheek before squaring my shoulders and getting my head in the game.

Opening my hand, I called back the sword I'd dropped earlier when I almost mutilated myself, feeling the weapons blend into my skin. *You got this, Charlie,* I told myself a few times while scanning the street. My eyes lifted up the tall building and past the few spotlights shooting sheets of yellow light skyward, until they stopped at a familiar window on the fifth floor.

My heart skipped a beat when the curtains that were pulled tightly over it shifted as if someone was peeking through them. With my heartbeat in my throat, I watched it unblinking, not daring to even breathe. Though when dark

The High Priestess

spots danced in front of my eyes I had no choice. Did that son of a cracked nut know I was here? If he did, would there be another trap waiting for me as soon as I dared step foot inside?

At this point, I was tapped-out and bone weary from everything, and the picture of the high priestess the night the book opened danced in front of my mind's eye. Every time I thought of that I remembered Selena perched on the window twirling the elder wood wand. It didn't make sense that she would be in the same bucket as the Magician, did it? She was helping Nigel get the book, wasn't she?

Nothing made sense.

All this was making me dizzy.

The pain in my hand was mostly gone, so I blew out a breath, shaking my palm as if I was trying to get rid of cobwebs that were stuck to it. My wrist cracked, the sound too loud to my ears in the sudden silence that blanketed the air around me. Freezing, I strained to hear the rustling of the leaves or the soft murmuring of the wind through the branches, but I was met with no luck. As if someone has pressed mute, the space around me continued the motions but nothing made a peep.

A tingling feeling started at my fingertips, and my heart raced, flipflopping wildly in my chest so hard my ribs hurt from it. Cold sweat trickled down my spine when numbness spread from my shoulders up the back of my neck, settling at the base of my skull. An invisible force pulled my gaze to the front entrance of the hotel, and my lips parted when two people walked out.

Jonas exited first, his head swiveling left and right as his dark, beady eyes scanned the street. After his perusal was complete, he moved to the side to hold the door open for the person behind him. Dressed in a smart suit with her hair tightly coiled in a bun at the base of her head, Selina stepped out with her shoulders back and her face an unreadable mask. She walked as if she was doing the cemented ground a favor by gracing it with her feet. I shrunk back further in the shadows, half hiding myself behind the trunk of the tree, and half praying that they wouldn't notice they were being watched. A million questions bombarded my brain, but none stayed long enough for me to grasp.

I watched as they stepped to the curb, and the black car glided smoothly in front of them. The back door opened while the vehicle was still moving, and Selena was already sliding inside it. As her head ducked in, I was about to move, but instead my fingers dug into the bark of the tree when Jonas's gaze snapped in my direction. *Please, look away. Please, look away...* my mind screamed. I might hate the mother trucker, but I wasn't ready to deal with him yet. The whispers that were constant in the back of my mind connecting me to the book intensified, humming insistently and bouncing through my panicked brain.

His eyebrows dipped low over his eyes, a line slicing between them while he blinked a few times and shook his head. My heart stopped when the hand he had pressed on the open door dropped to his side, but Jonas didn't come to investigate. With one last confused look my way, he followed Selena and disappeared inside the idling car. The vehicle peeled off the sidewalk flowing into the traffic until the back red lights blinked to life like demon's eyes when it stopped at the corner before taking a right.

I jumped a foot off the ground and twisted an ankle when the sound returned with a loud snap like a popping balloon. All the fudge in the world couldn't help while I jumped in a circle on one foot and gripped my sore ankle as

The High Priestess

if I was performing a tribal dance and calling the rain. Just a bonfire was missing to add to my embarrassment. Soft snickering came from behind me, but when I whirled around there was no one there.

"Great, Charlie. You are not just a clumsy dimwit, you're hearing things, too." Muttering under my breath, I pressed a thumb and a forefinger to the bridge of my nose, pressing hard enough for colors to burst behind my closed eyelids. "Which gods have I angered this time to be punished like this?"

"I might be able to help find which god if you tell me the punishment." A deep voice behind me spoke, which elicited a shrill squeak that ripped from my chest.

Magic burst from my fingertips, leaving black burn marks on the pavement.

I'd recognize that British accent anywhere, even if I was dead and hearing it from beyond the veil. Pressing my palm to the center of my chest to hold my heart inside my body, I spun around to glare and Nigel, the son of a cracked nut, Thatcher. The organ pumping blood through my body failed to do its job when my eyes landed on the bloodsucker. It stuttered weakly like the wings of a dying butterfly, fluttering against my ribs when those gray orbs that reminded me of a stormy sky locked on my face.

One side of his lips was cocked into a knowing smirk, which made a dimple form in his cheek. The corners of his eyes were slightly crinkled while he fought what looked like a laugh at my expense, and one lock of his carefully styled hair teased his forehead. Dressed in a button down shirt that looked painted on just to outline every ridge on his muscular torso, he had his hands tucked in his pants, which had an iron line in the middle of each leg sharper than my blades. If I didn't want to strangle him, I would've wondered if he was real or a product of my imagination. That thought snapped me out of my obvious gawking.

My left eye developed a twitch.

"Good evening, Ms. Jansen." A deaf person could hear the humor in the tone of his voice.

"Oh, look," I blurted the first thing that came to mind, "you're still alive."

"Were you worried about me, Ms. Jansen?"

"What? No!"

"If I knew you cared that much, I would've sent word." He was standing unnaturally still and doing that vampire thing he did, which only unnerved me further. "Did you come to check if I was well?"

"Don't flatter yourself you son of a cracked nut. I was …" My stupid heart drummed in my throat, while my mind worked overtime to come up with an excuse as to why I was standing like a creep across from his hotel. "I was going to the hotel."

"Oh?" Tilting his head, I couldn't even take a full breath as his knowing gaze pinned me. "To see me?" His smirk grew while I fumbled for an answer.

"Rabbits." Practically shouting the word in his face, I grinned like a fool when his eyebrows climbed up to kiss his hairline.

"Rabbits?" Nigel's chin dipped to his chest and he looked at me like I'd lost my mind.

"Huge ones." My brain and my mouth were not cooperating so everything that came out made me sound like a Neanderthal. "Blue. And a pink one, too. Glass."

Filling my lungs with so much air my chest hurt, I blew it out slowly through pursed lips, and Nigel watched me with concern twisting the features on his handsome face. My hands tingled from my anxiety, so when I wiped the

The High Priestess

sweaty palms off my thighs, I zapped myself with magic, releasing a strangled yelp. Nigel's lips parted, no doubt to ask if I needed a ride to a mental institution, but I beat him to it.

"I came because I wanted to see the glass rabbits in the hotel." He cocked one eyebrow as if he didn't believe a word I'd just said, but I didn't care. I was committed to the lie, now. "They left a big impression when I was in the hotel, so I'm here to see them again. Especially the blue and pink one. The large ones."

He blinked twice, much to my relief, but panic hit me when his gaze traveled from my face to my feet and back up. His eyes lingered on my thigh, and I wanted to kick myself. I forgot about stabbing my lag. He is a vampire, so of course he would know I had blood on me. I was proud that I didn't slap my forehead right then and there.

"Do you often bleed yourself before going to look at art, Ms. Jansen?" Suspicion slanted his eyes, and for the first time I felt his power tease my senses.

"It comes with the job." His gaze narrowed more, so I kept blabbing to distract him. "Bleeding, I mean. Not art."

"What job?"

"I'm an Assassin Mage … what do you mean 'what job?'" Frustration at myself, not him, infused my voice, but at least I wasn't using random words like "vomit".

Progress.

Nigel closed his eyes and released a heavy sigh. My stomach dropped to my feet. With a shake of his head, he speared his fingers through his hair before turning his back to me. My body was already moving in preparation to bolt out of there faster than I could say piñata, but his next words stopped me in my tracks.

"Let us move away from the open." Glancing over his

shoulder, I could see from his expression that he knew I was about to run. "We need to talk."

The bloodsucker didn't wait to see if I would follow, or even if I disagreed with his assessment of what *we* needed or didn't need. His long legs ate the distance, and he was across the street before I had a chance to argue. Clenching my fists, I drilled holes in his back with my glare while calling him every name under the sun in my head. I was one-hundred percent certain what I didn't need. I had no business being alone with Nigel Thatcher in a hotel room. Or a street, or a town, really. A continent between us wounld still be too close for comfort.

My feet, as if they had a mind of their own, rushed to guide me across the street where he was holding the door of the hotel open for me. "You are an idiot, Charlie," I hissed under my breath.

Nigel chuckled as he closed the door behind us.

Chapter Three

The confines of the elevator were pressing on me from all sides. I was too aware of Nigel next to me, although I kept my eyes focused on one spot on the closed doors so I didn't act on my impulse that was screaming at me to turn around and wrap myself around him like a baby koala. The elevator rocked when it came to a stop, causing the back of his hand to brush mine. Goosebumps spread from my wrist to my shoulder instantly.

"After you, Ms. Jansen." His palm popped into my field of vision, the other hovering behind me, so close I felt the heat from his skin through my shirt even though we weren't touching.

My molars cracked as I stepped out on the fifth floor, my boot catching on the tiny gap and pitching me forward stumble out. I could feel his smile burning between my shoulder blades, so I clenched my jaw so tight that a pain shot through the side of my face. I kept on grinding my teeth, though, remembering the white rose and his dimwitted behavior the night he'd taken blood from me. Marching down the hallway, I was getting increasingly frustrated with each stomp my boots made on the carpeted floor. More than anything, I was angry that he walked behind me so nonchalantly, as cool as a cucumber, even, while I felt like I would puke at any moment because of my swirling thoughts.

Nostrils flaring, I stared at the doorframe while waiting for him to swipe the card and let us in the room. After one beep and one flash of a green light, Nigel entered his room with me right on his heels, and when he flicked a switch, everything in the room was illuminated in a soft yellow glow. It should've been a different color. Some angry, sinister color rather than the golden light bathing everything around me. He paused in the middle of the room and turned to face me. As I watched his lips part, nervous energy swam through me because I knew he was about to speak, and if he did, the sound of his voice would scramble my brain, so I reacted on impulse.

I punched him.

My arm cocked before connecting with his jaw so hard he stumbled back a step, his head flying to the side. As my heart hammered my ribs, I stood frozen with one arm extended just to the side of his face, but all I could focus on were his wide eyes because they looked like they were ready to pop out of their sockets. I didn't move even when he straightened and rubbed his jaw with his strong fingers. If looks could kill, I was sure the skin on my face would've melted, but luckily for me all I had to endure was his furious glare.

"Are we done or should I ready myself for more fists flying?" The calm way he said that contradicted the silver shimmering through his gray irises.

The High Priestess

He looked feral.

Gulping, I retracted my arm and took a step back, just in case.

In case of what, I had no idea. The bloodsucker could move so fast no eyes could track him, but my stupid monkey brain had somehow made me believe that a couple of steps between us would keep me safe. My powers swirled at the center of my chest, a reminder that I had back up ... as unreliable as it was. It was still something, though, and something was better than nothing.

"We are done ... for now," I answered, and then his eyes narrowed. I immediately clamped my mouth shut.

When the silence stretched between us and reached uncomfortable levels, he spoke. "I believe you have questions."

"You think?"

"Sass will not take you far, Ms. Jansen." With a sigh, he moved to the desk stuck to the wall and perched on it, crossing one ankle over the other.

The room looked exactly the same as the night I was here to kill him. The piles of pillows pretending to be a person sleeping were missing, and the water stain from where I knocked the vase had been cleaned like it never existed. The plush carpet looked brand new, and maybe it was. The one good thing in the whole mess was the fact that I'd seen Selena with my own eyes leave the hotel. At least I didn't have to worry about her and that elder wood wand freaking me out from behind the closed curtains. Which reminded me.

"I see you and Jonas became buddies."

"I beg your pardon?"

"Don't pretend like you don't know what I'm talking about, Margie." Frowning at him, I balled my fists. "I saw

Jonas, a mage from my clan, come here and leave with Selena in tow a few minutes before you decided to scare the life out of me."

"I thought you came here to look at the rabbits, Ms. Jansen." The mocking way he said that set my teeth on edge.

I glared.

Scrubbing a hand over his face, Nigel pinched his chin and eyed me for a long moment. With a very ungraceful snort, he shook his head and chuckled without humor. By the expression on his face, I expected him to tell me to get the hell out of his face. Instead, his shoulders dropped, and I didn't miss the weariness tugging on his features, though it was the first time I'd seen anything like that on him.

"Master Bowman requested Selena's presence, so he sent one of his goons to collect her." Tucking his hands in his pockets, he paused as if he was debating something. After a few seconds, continued despite his earlier reluctance. "Apparently, in all the mess, no one saw me leave or found my dead body, though quite a few saw Selena at the mages guild that night. Your uncle sounded a little too worried about my wellbeing, and since I'd like to keep my status unknown for now, Selena went to reassure him that she hasn't seen or heard from me, but also to make sure he knew she was there trying to find me when she heard of an attack."

"There is no way word would've travelled that fast, no way she would've heard about it already to be there when it happened." I wanted to be proud that I found a hole in his plan, but it died a sudden death when a line formed between his eyebrows. "What? She couldn't have heard about it in the twenty, thirty minutes tops that it took the

The High Priestess

whole thing went down." A chill crawled up my spine and I shivered.

"What exactly happened on that floor, Ms. Jansen?"

"The Magician died, and I lived. That's what happened." His lips twisted in a grimace, which irked me. "You were there," I reminded him, speaking slowly like he was delayed in the ticker.

"I did not expect him to have that much power," Nigel murmured under his breath, but I could tell the words were more for himself than for me. His gaze grew distant, and I figured he was probably recounting that night. After a few moments passed, his sharp gaze focused on me once again. "How did you kill him? And where did you take his body?"

I blinked at him, though my mind screamed, *Oh, fudge. Mother fudge, I didn't think that far ahead. Run Charlie, run!*

With all the patience of a saint, he watched me intently, marking every breath I took and each blink of an eye. To buy some time and so I didn't bolt out of the room, I spun on my heel as if I was about to take a seat. Choosing to stick with the sass rather than telling him the truth, I flipped around and dropped on the bed with a ready-to-shoot smartass remark. I misjudged the distance—really, I'd never been good with depth perception—and my tailbone grazed the edge of the bed. My spine rattled when I dropped on the ground, and all the air swooshed out of my lungs with a loud "*Oomph.*"

Even through the rushing of blood in my ears, I heard Nigel's bark of laughter. My face burned hot in embarrassment. Mortified, I stayed mute when strong arms tucked under mine and lifted me before depositing me gently on the soft mattress. To his credit, the son of a cracked nut didn't laugh at me much more than the initial guffaw he'd released, though a few snickers escaped here and there. I could live with that.

"Are you alright, darling?" Tucking the hair behind my ear to see me better, he peered down at me.

"What did I say would happen if you called me darling one more time?" I grumbled, slapping his hands away.

"I see you are perfectly fine," Nigel drawled as he moved away from me, thank goodness. "Well? Where is his body? The guild was standing strong, with wards he'd erected around it. They collapsed at some point because there hasn't been a trace of them since that night. The only way that would happen was if he died."

"There is no body." My chin jutted out stubbornly in hopes he'd stop asking.

He didn't.

"What do you mean there is no body. He was a mage. There is always a body." Squinting at me, he waited. When I didn't speak, he kept poking. "Where is it?"

"Poof! Gone." Snapping at him, I grabbed fistfuls of the bed cover and strangled it. Of course, I imagined I held Nigel's neck between my strong grip, but he didn't need to know that. "I told you my magic is unpredictable. I blasted him head on. There was nothing left afterward. Poof…"

"Goodness gracious, you were telling the truth." His accent thick, he gawked at me as if I'd sprouted a second head.

"Of course I'm telling the truth." A weight lifted off my chest because he believed me, but it was short lived.

"You can't lie to save your life." Chuckling incredulously, he shook his head. "Un-bloody-believable."

"Wait, what?" My shoulders snapped back, and I watched him owlishly.

The High Priestess

He just kept snickering. "I can honestly say, Ms. Jansen, that I've never met anyone like you in my long life."

"What's that supposed to mean?"

"That is exactly what I'm trying to figure out, as well." As if he'd flipped a switch, all the humor left his face in an instant. "Where is the body?"

"There was no body after I killed him." There, that was the truth, although not the full story.

"How is that possible?" He was firing questions at me faster than bullets from a rifle.

"I honestly don't know how the body was not on that floor after he died." Another truth, and I kept praying he wouldn't ask me where it went. I had no idea how to get out of that one without him catching me in a lie.

"You are telling the truth."

"Don't act so surprised, you mother trucker. Of course I'm telling the truth. You sent me there with barely any useful information, and now you have the guts to question and lecture me about it? I could've died."

"Things didn't go as planned." Taken aback, he scowled at his shiny loafers. "He wasn't supposed to be aware that you were in that room until it was too late. I must've missed a ward ..." I felt bad for his shoes because he looked like he wanted to chew them off in his anger. "But there was no outside ward anywhere."

"Wait a minute ... you are telling me you've been to that room before and didn't take the book, but you sent me there on purpose? You were trying to get me killed?"

"Don't be absurd, Ms. Jansen. If all I wanted was your death, why would I send you to someone else? Especially when I could have the pleasure to kill you myself?"

"You tell me." My own anger returned, and I stood to him. "Why did you send me and not take it yourself?"

"I couldn't enter the room. It wouldn't open for me." If I was to describe the look on his face, I'd say it was accusatory. As if it was my fault he couldn't get in. "Very well. There is no body. Where is the book?"

"Umm ..."

"Ms. Jansen." I'd never heard so much warning packed into someone saying my name. It promised all sorts of pain if I attempted to lie again.

I didn't lie.

I said nothing.

Zipping my mouth shut, I stared dumbly at him like I didn't speak the language he spoke and couldn't understand the question. A vein started throbbing in his temple, and a muscle jumped on one side of his jaw. The silence stretched so long I expected us to stay like that for days without one of us even blinking. If the vampire thought he would wear me down, he had another thing coming. I had every intention of staying mute for as long as it took, and I'd just have to pray I didn't have to pee. That was my plan anyway, until he stiffened and his head snapped to the side where the tall windows covered the wall.

My heart lodged in my throat.

"What's wrong?" If I sounded shaky it was because my voice carried my heartbeat with it.

"You need to go." Springing into action, he snatched my upper arm and started dragging me to the door.

With my mouth hanging open in shock, I watched as he opened the door, stuck his head out, and looked around. Only then did he turn to face me. Displeasure was plastered in every line of his face, but he managed to grind the words out.

"Selena is back. Go left and take the stairs, do you understand?"

Nodding like a dimwit, I shouldered my way past him and was about to turn left and sprint for freedom when his soft words made me stumble a step.

"This is not over, Ms. Jansen." Nigel's voice washed over me like a caress. "I'll see you soon."

I could've sworn I felt his eyes on me half way through the city.

Chapter Four

I was trotting across the parking lot in front of Tia's building when it hit me. Why in the world did Nigel ask me to leave so Selena didn't see me? Aren't they working together? Wasn't figuring out where the book was more important than whatever reason he wanted me to stay away from her? He hadn't been concerned about my safety, or my life for that matter, when he sent me to steal for him, so why was he interested in keeping me alive now? Questions continued to pile up in my already exhausted brain until I couldn't even focus to walk in a straight line.

My feet were barely off the stairs on Tia's floor when her door was yanked open and I was greeted by her scrunched-up face. While she had one hand firmly on her hip and one foot tapping as if she wanted me to know how unhappy she was with me at the moment, her eyes were busy shooting arrows at my forehead. I could even, theoretically, see them stabbing at the center.

"Oh, look," she drawled, glancing over her shoulder at

The High Priestess

who I assumed was Glenda hovering behind her. "If it isn't miss 'I work alone so get away from me.'"

"Can we not do this, please." With a heavy sigh, I shouldered my way inside her apartment. "If I say sorry, will you drop it?"

"No." Sniffing, she closed the door and locked it behind her.

"I didn't think so." Muttering under my breath, I paused midstride to take in the living room without fainting from the mix of colors that were making my head spin every time I walked inside the place.

Lo and behold, I was right. Glenda stood in the middle of the rainbow-colored room twisting her fingers into pretzels in front of her, and she was looking everywhere but at my face. The splash of random, clashing colors hit me like a punch to the face every time I saw them, and tonight was no exception. I had to stop to allow my brain time to adjust so I didn't take a nosedive into a piece of furniture. Since they both hadn't changed from their spy attire, as Tia had dubbed it, all three of us were dressed in all black, and we all stood out like dark smudges in an abstract painting of an artist high on hallucinogenic drugs. Glenda and I spent most of our lives surrounded by black and gray, washed-out, unassuming colors, and things that drew no attention. It was like stepping into a different world when we entered Tia's land of bright colors. Well, it was for me. The seer did wear colors here and there, though I suspected that only happened when she wanted to hide the bruises after an encounter with Jonas, or another dimwit from our clan.

"It takes some getting used to, huh?" Glenda peered at me from under her lashes, her face pinking slightly at the cheekbones. The timid woman grew a spine occasionally, which made me proud, sure, but it seemed to take a while for her to break out of her shell.

On the bright side of things, no one would be able to break into this rabbit hole "Alice in Wonderland" style and steal the Necronomicon. Their heads would be spinning so much we would find them still unconscious days later. A perfect hiding spot if ever I saw one.

"Well?" Tia snapped from behind me, ignoring both our reactions to her interior design skills. "Why do you look like you've seen a ghost after he pinched your ass?"

"A what?" I did that a lot around Tia. I was always left wondering if I heard her right or if she was speaking in tongues, and I definitely always felt like an idiot because I never understood even her simplest questions.

"What happened, Charlie?" Pronouncing each word slowly, she shook her head at me on her way to the sofa, plopping on it from a foot up. She didn't bounce, which was a testament to how uncomfortable those sofas were to sit on. Not that I'd ever dare tell her that.

With great reluctance, I joined them, gingerly lowering my still-smarting tush from the miscalculation in Nigel's hotel room on it. Rubbing my forehead to buy time and phrase what I needed to say correctly, I peeked at her through my fingers.

"I saw Nigel." She took a big breath, so I rushed forward to finish before Tia bombarded me with a million rapid-fire questions, watching Glenda from the corner of my eye move from where she was still standing to join the human on the sofa across from me. "Jonas left the hotel with Selena in tow before the son of a gun came downstairs and scared the living hell out of me just to make sure I knew he was aware I'd been there the whole time." An unseemly snort passed Glenda's lips at my choice of swearing, but she sobered up pretty fast after a sharp look from me. Pressing my lips together in frustration, I rubbed my palms on my thighs to wipe off the sweat. "Which was one of the reasons I didn't want the two of you anywhere near that place. We know nothing about the bloodsucker apart from how vicious he is when it comes to his identity. I have no doubt in my mind that hasn't changed just because I got shackled to a book that was supposed to be a myth. If anything, I think he will be more adamant to keep his face a secret, now more than ever."

"Lecture us later, after you are done telling us what happened." Her mouth twisted in a grimace, Tia swirled her hand at me in an "out with it" gesture. "I have questions."

"I don't think you should ask her anything tonight." Glenda was staring wide-eyed at my fingers, and to my horror I realized tiny sparks of magic were popping out of my fingertips.

"I have it under control." I had absolutely nothing under control. I just didn't want them freaking out and thinking I was about to burn the building down, so I balled my fists until my nails dug holes in the skin of my palms. "He wanted me to follow him to his room because talking about everything in the open was not smart." It was Tia who snorted in disbelief this time, but I spoke over it, although my face got really hot.

Mother fudging bloodsucker with his dimwitted British accent.

"He is pushing to know where the body of The Magician is, as well as the location of the book." Rattled by the events that took place in the mages guild that night, I told Glenda and Tia everything when we came to this apartment. Knowing the story, they both blanched at what I just told them. "I told him the body of the son of a cracked nut disappeared. One second there, the next, *poof*, it was gone."

"Oh my God! She lied." Tia slapped a hand on her forehead, while Glenda was groaning like she had food poisoning. "Tell me what you said, word for word. I'll be able to tell if it worked."

"He didn't believe me," I told my self-professed lie detector with a glare.

"Obviously, since we didn't practice—"

"So I stuck to the truth, just not all of it." I spoke over her before she proceeded to throw more insulting comments my way. Honestly, I just wanted to get it all out and be done talking. A headache had started throbbing at my temples, which told me I needed to get away from everyone, but I knew it was from the constant whispers of the book, which had grown to the point of deafening since I was in such close proximity to it. "I said I had no idea where the body went, which was the truth. I still don't know what happened and how it was possible. It's all a blur of disbelief ... mostly."

"And the book?" Glenda asked softly. Tia just pouted and crossed her arms across her chest for being silenced before she was done.

"I got lucky about that ... I think." A frown scrunched my forehead as I stared at my feet and tried to process what exactly had happened before I bolted out of the bloodsucker's room. "I panicked when he asked about the book. I wasn't ready for a recount of my events with Nigel. I just wanted to know if he was still alive." Locking my gaze with Glenda, my belly tightened at the pity I saw there. Not that I blamed her. I was a pitiful excuse for an Assassin Mage. "He sprang into action out of nowhere in the middle of drilling me, telling me Selena was back and I

The High Priestess

needed to take the stairs to get out of there so she didn't see me."

"Isn't she helping him?" Tia forgot she was upset with me as she leaned forward on the sofa. "Why would he hide you from her? Selena is the one with the stick, right?" She turned to Glenda in question.

"A wand," the seer corrected her, though her eyes never left me. "Yes, that's her." I could see the same wariness I felt reflected on Glenda's face. We were both thinking about the open book and the picture of the High Priestess staring at us from the floor.

But it didn't make sense.

Why would Selena be in the same pot with The Magician? As far as I was aware, she was Nigel's right hand and helped him get whatever it was he wanted in the moment. Which could be world domination for all I knew, and if it was, I really didn't care. What didn't sit well with me was the fact that I was apparently hiding from her now. The memory of the elder wood wand sent a shiver over my whole body, which made me look like a dog trying to shake off fleas.

"It's a stick," Tia informed us primly, but I was glad for her in that moment because she put a stop to the turbulent thoughts trying to take over my mind. Though when her words registered, I blinked at her stupidly. "What? I googled it and it looks like a stick to me." She shrugged as if completely unperturbed by us gaping at her. "I can carve one out myself and wave it around Harry Potter style, too. It doesn't change the fact that it's a stick."

"Well, this *stick*"—Stabbing a finger in her face so she paid attention, I made sure she understood the danger—"will make finding the pieces of you with a microscope difficult. Stay away from Selena, Tia. I'm not joking."

"I need a drink." Tia paled before jumping to her feet and darting in the kitchen. "I'll become an alcoholic in no time around you," she called, her voice muffled while she rummaged through her refrigerator. "Aha! I knew you were here, my love."

We watched her mutely when she returned cradling a very large bottle to her chest as if someone might take it. It must be the "love" she had referred to a second ago, so we tracked her when she deposited it on the low coffee table and scuttered to bring three glasses, dumping them next to it with a resounding cling.

"You gulp tequila like it's water. Don't blame it on me," I muttered as I watched her wrestle the cap of the bottle with her teeth in fascination. She stilled her shaking head to turn a startled gaze at me, the huge bottle looking like a flute sticking out of her mouth.

"Ever since I've been friends with you, I have been drinking." She poked the air in my direction with an accusing finger and my spine stiffened. "I knew something was off, but I couldn't figure out what and it was eating me alive. Now I know why. Besides, it helps with the nightmares, too." That last part was more to herself, but as curious as I was about the nightmares she kept mentioning, I wasn't ready to talk about that yet.

"Blame it on me if it's easier." I hated that I was getting defensive, but knowing I was responsible for ruining my friend's life didn't sit well with me. Regardless of my grumbling, I still took the filled glass she shoved at me with narrowed eyes. "If it knocks you out so you can't follow me around, I'm all for it. Blame away, girl."

"You are not that lucky," Tia said in a dry tone, and then she brought the glass to her lips. "I'll drag my ass if I have to, but I'll be there to have your back. It's what side-

The High Priestess

kicks do." Sucking in air to argue, the words got stuck on my tongue. "Even those without magic. I can swing a baseball bat with the best of them. You people are so used to your powers and magic that no one will see a large chunk of wood coming at their face. Screw sticks and wiggling fingers. Meet Tia, the human swinging for a home run."

"You are talking nonsense," I said.

"She does have a good point, though," Glenda chirped, holding her glass with both hands like it was a holy grail. "Anyway, now what? We just hide here until we figure out what to do next?"

"Hell no." The yet-undiscovered baseball player nudged her with her hip. "I say we stalk those two and figure out their game."

"Which part of 'he knew I was outside the hotel and across the street' didn't you understand? Stalking doesn't work that way." The headache had gotten worse, and my stomach had started churning and I tasted acid in the back of my throat.

"For you." Tia leaned back on the sofa, a smile stretching wide on her lips. "Just like you, they don't think highly of humans. We are nonexistent to them. That's where sidekicks come in."

"You are not going anywhere near them." I wanted to sound stern, but my words were slurring.

"What's wrong with her?" Tia's panicked voice was coming from somewhere far away while my vision tunneled to a pinprick.

"I think the bond with the book is overwhelming her." Glenda sounded like she was talking underwater. "Take her glass, I got her."

I felt nothing, although blurry shapes were moving around me. The whispers were now screaming as if determined to be heard, and they were pulling at me to join them in their abyss of misery. The room tilted and my eyes rolled to the back of my head, but I could've sworn I heard Tia speak.

"You look after her. I'll be back as soon as I can."

My brain was screeching for her to stay where she was, my thoughts joining Glenda's verbal protests, but I heard the front door close just as I lost consciousness. My soul would burn for eternity if anything happened to my stubborn friend.

Chapter Five

Sweat was trickling down to my neck from both sides of my face and plastering my hair to my skin. Hot air burned my throat with each inhale, while I struggled to open my eyes to see where I was. Last time I checked, I hadn't gone to any saunas, nor was I in the middle of a burning building, but the way my life had been going lately, I wasn't that excited to find out what new hell I'd conjured up for myself this time. So I stayed as I was and wiggled my fingers to get the feeling back in my arms. Then I was gasping for air and all memories of how I'd ended up here vanished.

At least it was quiet.

As soon as that thought came I wanted to slap myself. I'd never learned not to tempt Karma, the ever-vigilant prover of wrong when it came to me. Leaves rustled and the crack of a branch boomed so loud in my ears I felt like I was standing in the epicenter of an explosion. With my mouth open in a silent scream from the pain, I writhed on the unforgiving ground while wishing I was dead. As the agony abruptly ended, an even worse feeling spread through me when a foot scraped the ground coming from the side, way too close for comfort.

My heart punched me in the throat and jammed there like it had become an enormous fist that was trying to choke me, and all my blood curdled in my veins. The tiny survival instinct I had reared its head to inform me that I was in grave danger. As much as I wanted to open my eyes and see what I'd gotten myself into, I kept them tightly shut, scrunching my face as if that would make whoever it was go away. If I couldn't see them, they couldn't see me either, right? In the crippling fear crawling under my skin, that was my logic, though I knew it was incredibly flawed.

Stupid, even.

Summoning everything in me, I knew I was playing possum. Ungluing my eyelashes, I pried my eyes apart just enough to peek without being noticed. They hadn't attacked yet, and I knew without a doubt that if they wanted me dead, I would have been many times by now. Buying more time by staying still, my mind spun with one thought after another about how I might get myself out of whatever situation this was. Every idea came and went before I could grasp it, my brain dismissing all the dimwitted ways I wanted to go about it. Screaming or running for it never worked for anyone, so it wasn't about to start with me.

Darkness met my slanted gaze, and it was broken only by the faint glow of an orange orb high above my head. I realized I was facing the sky, which extended as far as my vision permitted me to see. Deeper shades to my right reached for the million stars like some jacked-up teeth, and it reminded me of stacked rocks instead of a high hill that it was supposed to be. A glint between them made my heart stutter in my chest, and then bright orange eyes glanced at but disappeared so fast I wasn't sure if they were a product

The High Priestess

of my imagination or not. As afraid as I was, I knew how easy it would be for my mind to conjure all sorts of monsters lurking in the shadows around me.

"You are here much sooner than those before you." A voice so deep I could feel it vibrating in my chest through the hard-packed ground spoke, the sound of grinding rocks prickling my skin and covering it in chills and cold sweat. "I cannot be sure if that makes you stronger than your predecessors, or if it is a sign that you need to be disposed of so a stronger one can take your place." As much as I didn't want to see who it was, my head turned toward the voice, though I dreaded coming face to face with the person talking. "Do not gaze upon me, sentinel, for I need you sane ... until I have decided your fate."

Numb from being terror stricken, I held my breath and froze. The petrifying laugh coming from the person that spoke shook the ground, and a fresh wave of emotions spread through my entire body. Fury burned all the fear I had when the son of a nut chortled because he knew I was scared. What a bully. And bullies were one thing that threw all my logic and self-preservation to the side. My fists clenched and my jaw tightened hard, grinding my teeth.

"Where am I?" His snickering stopped the second I spoke. "How did I get here?"

Trusting his warning not to look at him—for now—I rolled to my side and pushed off the ground while keeping my gaze down. The density of the air around me changed, his curiosity saturating each of my breaths while I scrubbed a forearm across my forehead to wipe the salty sweat that was stinging my eyes.

"Well?" Blind and idiotic in my rage, I snapped at him. "The cat got your tongue, or do you talk only when you want to scare people, boogeyman? Where am I?"

He stayed silent, although I felt his intent stare like the sharp point of a sword poking me in the side of the face. To remove the temptation of returning the favor and facing him, I lifted my gaze and blinked at the sky. The next breath stuck halfway in my lungs when I saw the largest moon I'd ever seen in my life hanging so low above my head I had no doubt I'd touch it with my fingertips if I reached for it. If the size wasn't an indication I was no longer home, the color of it was a dead giveaway. The burnt orange color glowed at me, with streaks of deep red, gold, and electric blue zipping through it like lightning strikes without the thunder. Forgetting all the fear and anger, I gawked at it in fascination. I'd never seen something so beautiful and so terrifying at the same time.

"Oh, oh." I breathed under my nose. "Houston, we have a problem."

"To whom do you speak? You came here alone." Tremors raked me from the rage in his deep voice.

"It's a figure of speech, you mother trucker," I blurted through numb lips. "Where am I?" My fingers were twisting in the fabric of my pants, more to stop myself from running than anything else.

"It's the realm of the gods, sentinel." White noise filled my ears when I heard him shift from behind me, and then goosebumps popped all over my skin. "I take it you did not intend to be here."

"You think?" Biting hard on my tongue to stop talking, I tasted the coppery blood before it trickled down my throat.

His laughter made me stumble, and then my arms were windmilling to keep my balance while I waved left and right like a drunk going home at four in the morning from the pub. He kept at it until my knees buckled, and then I dropped on them. In the process, I scraped the crap out of my skin and ripped my pants. My palms slid across sharp, tiny rocks until they were shredded like paper and I unwillingly gifted the dry dirt with my blood. A groan from the dimwit blasted my eardrums, though it did scare the daylights out of me. Deep in my soul I knew I'd messed up by bleeding, but there was nothing I could do about it. Tentatively, I lifted on my knees and fisted my hands.

"No sentinel has given a gift of life without asking for something in return." Suspicion was clear in his rumbling voice, but his words only induced more panic inside of me. "What do you want?"

"To go home?" It came out as a squeak.

Silence.

It stretched so long I almost turned to glance over my shoulder to make sure he hadn't left me there to fend for myself. Then I thought maybe I'd be the next snack for some nightmarish creature or something, but the scrape of a pebble told me he was still there, so I stayed facing forward and kneeling on the ground as if preparing to be executed.

"You are a strange creature, sentinel," he muttered, his hot breath blasting the side of my face when he spoke from right behind me.

My heart stopped.

"My name is Ulthar. I am the guide to the Great One, and you are in Betelgeuse, the star on which we live ... for now."

"Can I go home?" I hated how my lips trembled and my voice shook because it made me sound like a frightened little girl.

"You are the sentinel, which means you can come and go as you please." Amusement colored his words. "It was you who came here this night. You were not summoned. It stands to reason that you can also leave, no?"

"How do I do that?" Swallowing thickly, I figured I had nothing to lose by asking since he was being so chatty. "I can't remember how I got here."

"A very peculiar creature indeed, sentinel." My spine stiffened when he took a strand of my matted hair and rubbed it between his fingers. "You have but to wish yourself in this realm for you to pass the gate. You are the guardian of the Gate of the Gods, after all. You have the power to keep it open or to close it. A word of advice from me, sentinel, would be tread carefully so as not to abuse that power. None of us look kindly on those who try to use us as pawns. We feast on the bones of any who have tried."

"You mean the book? The Necronomicon?" Wetting my dry lips with the tip of my tongue, I took a moment to chew on his words in the hopes I'd understand what he was saying. "That's the gate I can close and open?"

"The book, as you call it, is the sacred text of our world" He tugged on the hair he was still holding, ripping a strand off my scalp. I was so numb from fear that I barely felt the sting, though my heard definitely skipped a beat or two. "Guard it with your life, sentinel, for if another takes control of it, they can use it against you … and as things stand for the time, I'm growing rather fond of you. You amuse me. Which brings me to an urgent matter you need to be aware of."

"No one is taking the book." The words were jumbled as they poured from my lips in a rush.

"That is your path to take, and I cannot help you with it." My body jerked in surprise when he answered, although I had rudely cut him off. "Before the bond formed between our world, the one who controlled the gate made a mess of

The High Priestess

things." My hair whipped around to slap my face when he released a sigh from what felt like a blasting wind surging around us. "He left the gate open for a short time while he attempted to inform us that he had the control of our lives and we needed to do his bidding. Fool."

Horror sunk its claws in my lungs until it felt like they were torn to shreds, and his chuckle only deepened the gashes. Barely any breath stayed in me at the sound because it reminded me of a nightmare.

"The Magician," I breathed through unmoving lips.

"Ah, yes. The Magician, he called himself. Rather fitting for his end. Don't you agree, sentinel?"

"What happened to him, to the body? The card ..." I trailed off, too busy twisting my fingers in the fabric of my pants to continue. He didn't answer for so long I thought he had left and then finally, he spoke. "Perhaps another time, sentinel. The time is short and you have stayed here too long. Be aware when the gate was opened that a priestess of Nodens snuck through into the world. One of his three mates. A rather mischievous creature, she is, that Nira. Be that as it may, the Lord of the Abyss wants her back, and you need to help guide her through the gate."

"Me?" My heartbeat was in my throat, and my body had started shivering at the idea of me chasing nightmarish creatures through the world. "I hate to break the news to you, but I'm not exactly that competent when it comes to staying out of trouble—or alive if you want to get technical. How in the world will I make a priestess do what I tell her? I can't make Tia the human do what I ask." That last part was more to me than to him.

"You are a descendent of a strong bloodline, sentinel. Don't repeat the mistakes of your foremothers. They fought their destiny and it cost them their lives. Do not do the same. The Fates will guide those who will help you across your path, but it is up to you to recognize them. It is time for you to leave, so don't waste time. Find Nira and send her back before Nodens comes to fetch her himself. It won't be good for anyone if he walks through the gate now."

"How will I find her? I don't even know what she looks like? Or what to look for."

"She will not show her true face to the human realm. If she does, chaos will swallow your world. No, she will bond with a strong magic user and use the human to do her bidding. Nira is young, the youngest of the three. She will have fun, as you humans like to call it. Now leave, do your duty, and bring her home."

"Hey, wait." A strong tug at the center of my chest made me sway on my feet, and I struggled to keep myself where I was. "I have more questions. Can she kill me? How do I kill her first if she tries to kill me?" Everything rushed out in one breath, but the dark world and the orange moon continued to spin in front of my eyes.

"She will either leave on her own or you will have to kill the host, sentinel. You will know when the time comes. It's what you were born to do."

His deep, scary voice was coming from the distance as my eyelids grew heavy and I started sinking toward the ground. I didn't realize at first that it was because my knees were giving out. I was panicking because I didn't get enough information to go on, but a cold hand took hold of my shoulder, drawing me from my alarm and snapping my head to the side. Translucent skin with a light bluish tint met my gaze, causing my brain to screech to a halt. Long bony fingers with too many joints to be human curled all the way to my collarbone. Pointy, dagger-like black nails left dents just above my poor boob, which seemed to be trying to shrink into my chest to escape the assault. Dark green veins shimmered under the membrane like skin. I couldn't comprehend what I was seeing, and I tried to fire a million questions. My lips parted to ask, but each word died on my tongue when darkness pulled me under and wiped my head clean.

"We will meet again soon, sentinel." His deep voice straight from the inside of a nightmare followed me into oblivion.

Chapter Six

"Jellyfish!"

I woke up screeching that word while my legs were jack-knifing, and I barely missed headbutting Tia, who was leaning over me, as I jerked up from her sofa.

She jumped away while screaming.

A shrill, ear-piercing noise rang through the room, and it felt like I was standing directly under a church bell as someone slammed it with a mother-fudging hammer. And the minute Tia's bellow shot through the air like she'd just turned into an opera singer with such a high pitch she had the power to shatter glass, Glenda did the same. The seer yelled from the top of her lungs, and I could see the little tear-shaped uvula trembling at the entrance of her throat when my startled gaze darted to her face.

I screamed, too.

I had absolutely no idea why they were screaming, I didn't think I'd scared them that much when waking up, but maybe I had and this was their kneejerk reaction. A few

The High Priestess

minutes passed while all three of us screamed, one after another like an acapella band made of dimwits.

"Why the hell are you screaming?" When reason finally won, I pressed a hand to the center of my chest to keep my hammering heart from punching a hole through my ribs.

"I thought you were dead." Tia glared at me and pointed an accusing finger at my face. "And who the fuck wakes up yelling 'jellyfish' of all things?"

"Monsters. The book." The memory from everything that happened slammed into me like a battering ram. "It's a gate to nightmares. The moon was orange and huge with lightning ..."

"Hold on, hold on." Tia excitedly rushed to my side, perching on the sofa next to me. "Start from the beginning and don't leave anything out."

Flaring my nostrils, I slowed my frantic breathing and told them everything that happened. The human grew more enthusiastic with each word, while Glenda was getting paler and paler by the second. I doubted a drop of blood was left in her face by the time I finished.

"I couldn't remember what his skin reminded me of until it finally hit me. Unfortunately, that was when I woke up, so I shouted jellyfish out loud, and well, we all know what happened after that." Sagging into the hard sofa, I rubbed a hand over my face. "What a disaster. If it's true and The Magician really did release a creature from that place into our world, I don't know how the humans haven't started a witch hunt by now. No offense Tia, but your kind does crazy things for a lot less."

"None taken, I'm used to you saying dumb shit by now." She waved a hand between us as if she was chasing flies with her face shoved in her phone, while I only gaped at her. "What I want to know, however, is when did he release her, this priestess he told you about?"

"Does it matter?" I asked incredulously.

Out of all the things to worry about, the timing was the least important one. Mr. Jellyfish was very clear that a scarier thing would be coming if we didn't send Nira back. I had every intention of doing everything in my power to prevent that from happening. Regardless if I liked it or not, being bonded to that cursed book left the responsibility in my hands.

"To you?" Cocking one eyebrow, she looked up from her phone screen. "No. To me, on the other hand, it matters a little too much."

"What are you talking about? Not the sidekick nonsense again, please." Rolling my eyes, I huffed at Glenda, who was still standing in the middle of the living room. She was as pale as the first snow. "Sit down before you drop like a rock. You're scaring me."

"Right," the seer muttered before she plummeted in a heap where she stood. "Sit down. Yes, that's a very good idea." Swallowing thickly, she fidgeted with the fabric of her shirt.

"You okay?" Worried for her mental state, I watched her like a hawk.

"I'm great," she squeaked a bit too brightly, and I frowned at her.

"Of course she's not okay, dumbass. Did you hear yourself when you told us what happened, about the creature roaming around?" Tia snapped from my side.

"I was there," I told her dryly. "I'm well aware of what happened."

"Well"—Ignoring my comment, she waved her phone at me—"according to the all-knowing God Google, Nodens is one of the old Gods, Lord of the Abyss. And all these creatures are monsters that control nightmares, literally. Which to me explains a lot of things, and that was why I wanted to know when this Nira entered our world. Because it would explain why I started drinking just so I could sleep without dreaming."

"Your nightmares." Glenda became animated again, and a little color returned to her face. "It is possible that the two are connected."

"I have no clue what the two of you are talking about and what that has to do with Nira." Confused, I glanced from Tia to Glenda and back.

"I've had nightmares on and off lately, though before that I rarely dreamed," Tia mumbled, staring at her hands. "It could explain why if they started around the same time this Nira person entered our world. As I said, it says here they are creatures of nightmares. They control our dreams and can physically hurt us through them, too."

"What?" Recoiling at the thought, I stared openly at her. "It can't be true. Please tell me it's not true." Two grim faces stared back at me. "Why is this happening to me?" I groaned and sunk back in hopes to disappear into the sofa.

I wasn't that lucky.

"I would ask what this is trying to teach you." Glenda spoke softly as she climbed to her knees. "There is a reason why the book chose you to bond with, Charlie. You said it yourself ... Ulthar kept calling you sentinel. If I'm being honest here, if anyone has control over a gate that leads to a land of monsters, I can't think of a better person to guard it other than you."

"She has a point," Tia chirped, perking up. "Out of all the people I've met, you are the one who isn't hungry power, so you have no nefarious motivations to use the book. As long as we keep you from tripping over your own feet and no one hears you swearing, you'll do just fine. Lucky for you, you have me as a sidekick. I'll do the talking and swearing for you since I'm a pro, and Glenda is your personal window to the future. You got this girl."

"You are forgetting one very important fact, oh wise ones." My anger was aimed at myself for getting mixed up in this shitstorm. "The book didn't choose squat. It was that son of a cracked nut that forced me to go fetch it for him. Remember the bloodsucker? That's who I have to thank for being shackled guarding gates that lead to monsters."

"As much as I want to agree with you, I think you are wrong." I turned a glare on Glenda, but instead of cowering like she usually did, she squared her shoulders stubbornly. "I've heard the stories about the murder of your parents. No one dared speak out loud about it, but the whispers that your mother was known as the Necronomicon guardian never died down. Some say it's a myth, the book, but we know better, don't we? I think whatever his reason, Nigel Thatcher nudged you in the right direction to your destiny."

"Don't romanticize the titty chomper just because he is hot." Clenching my fists, I desperately tried to dispute her claims.

"He really is a hottie. I would climb him like a tree given a chance."

"He wanted the Necronomicon for the Fates know what." Ignoring Tia's comments so I didn't zap her with magic, I stayed focused on Glenda. "There is a reason why all of us fear Nigel Thatcher and why no one, until now, knew his face. Don't think for a second he has some noble plan to guide little ol' me to some made up fairytale destiny."

"I never said that." Not backing down, she kept her

The High Priestess

gaze locked on mine. "All I'm saying is that everything happens for a reason and we are all pawns in the web of life. Whatever his plan was, it brought us all to the present moment it time. I feel it deep in my soul that you were born for this, Charlie. Don't fight against Fate, go with it. Nothing good comes from swimming upstream."

"This is why I stay away from everyone." Grumbling, I kept glaring, but the fire was missing in my voice. "I hate it when you make sense, Glenda."

"Look at you, I'm so proud." Tia beamed at me. "You told someone they were right and you survived. They grow up so fast." She batted her eyelashes at Glenda, which made the seer snort.

"Not funny."

"A little funny," she informed me, jutting her chin out.

"You know, Charlie, all this kind of makes sense in a creepy way, and it sets you on a clear path forward." The humor evaporated from Glenda's face when those knowing eyes of hers zeroed in on me. My stomach clenched. "You said Ulthar called Nira a priestess of Nodens, right?"

"I was scared out of my mind, but yes, I believe that's what he said." Racking my brain, I struggled to remember and goosebumps popped all over my arms. "It was hard to hear him clearly from the whooshing in my ears."

"And before you lost consciousness, when you saw Nigel, he sent you away so Selena didn't see you. I wonder if that's somehow connected and he felt something was off with her?" the seer mused. "If Nira needs a magic user as a host, the strongest one she could find would be one who can wave an elder wood wand like it's a regular stick."

My mouth opened to argue, but it closed with an audible snap.

"If that's true, she was a host before I bonded with the

Necronomicon. Before that bloodsucker sent me to steal it." I gnawed on my lower lip so much I was making a bloody mess of it. "She would've done anything to stop me from reaching it. I think you are wrong on this."

"Hmm, I think not." Tia slapped my thigh with the back of her hand. "Didn't you say the hottie told you the bad guy wasn't supposed to be aware you were in that room when he came to fight you? What if she couldn't do anything without outing herself, so she told him to expect you in hopes that he would kill you, that way no one would know she was prancing around making all of us miserable with no sleep?"

"The two of you are making it sound as if this was a big conspiracy theory to get Charlie killed. I doubt I even registered on their radar as being alive until I bonded with that cursed book." Not even I believed my words, but I wanted them to be true with everything in me.

"Yet you were given the impossible mission to kill the strongest vampire in the world as your first target while he tricked you to steal the Necronomicon for him," Glenda deadpanned with a straight face. "Want to try convincing us again with something else?" I hid my face in my hands, breathing in and out slowly so I didn't puke. "Do you remember where the book opened before we left the mages guild?"

"How can I forget?" Voice muffled through my fingers, I kept my eyes squeezed shut. "I don't want any part of this."

"I know, Charlie." The sadness in Glenda's words brought tears to my eyes. "But none of us can escape our fate, no matter what it is. What we can do is take the wheel and steer it in the direction we want it to go. We are creators of our own lives, after all. We just pick up the hand we are dealt and bluff our way through it the best we can."

"When did you become so wise?" Peeking at her through my hands, I couldn't help but smile. "I liked you better when you were timid and silent."

"When my friend's life depends on my wisdom." No humor reached her eyes even though she smiled back.

"What?"

"I became wise because that it's just another weapon we can use to keep you alive." Determination burned in her dark, forest eyes. "I'll be damned if I sit back and watch you die, Charlie. I'm going to scratch their eyes out. They want a piece of you? They'll have to go through me first. It's my turn to protect you the best way I know how."

"Hell, yeah," Tia joined in, making me jump when she spoke loudly from beside me. "Through me, too. Those fuckers will have no idea what hit them."

"Now what?" fighting the tears threating to spill, I dropped my hands in my lap and fought to push down the lump that formed in my throat.

"Now we do the stalking." Tia jumped to her feet. "Since we are keeping you out of sight, I'll take the bitch with the stick. Glenda can have the hottie."

My groan was followed by giggles from both of them.

Chapter Seven

"This is a very bad idea."

Two days we sulked outside of the hotel, watching the comings and goings like some creeps. In all that time, Jonas came once more, but no one left with him. It was a bust. We had no important information and had wasted precious time. Apart from not having a clue if we were correct about Selena, I was starting to think there was something going on between Jonas the dimwit and her, especially since his hair was all mussed when he left the hotel in a rush. For a reason I refused to name, that idea pleased me greatly. It had nothing to do with the fact I suspected that Nigel and Selena might be more than just working together. I disliked the son of a gun with everything in me, although my body and hormones hadn't gotten that memo.

"It's a great idea," Tia answered me, not taking her eyes off the road. "Trust me, no one will recognize us. I got you, boo."

Pursing my lips, I looked over my shoulder from the passenger seat at Glenda. The blonde wig and brown

The High Priestess

contact lenses Tia made her wear transformed the seer into a woman I'd never met before. The disguise worked great on Glenda. On both of them really. On me, however ...

The red wig and emerald contacts paired with the too-tight black dress that was pushing my boobs into my mouth made me look hideous. Tia, with straight black hair and her usual barely-there attire—just enough to cover the important bits—looked like a runway model. I looked like a hooker.

A cheap one at that.

"The bouncers will let the two of you in, and they'll kick me out. You watch." Tugging on the bottom of my dress, which was more like a longer tank top than anything else, I wiggled in the car seat.

"Knock it off, Charlie, you look great." Taking a sharp turn hard enough my head bounced off the window, Tia skidded into the parking lot of The Cauldron.

A line stretched around the building of people dressed in their best chatting excitedly while waiting for their turn to enter the club. Taking hold of the thick mesh coverup I was allowed to wear so I could cover my markings, I pulled my sleeves over my knuckles, chewing a hole on the inside of my mouth. I wished the damn coverup was closed at the chest to hide my boobs. Having them on display made me very uncomfortable. More than I liked to admit.

"Okay, remember your tasks." Tia the drill sergeant parked as far from the entrance as possible, killing the engine. "Chat with anyone willing to talk and ask about nightmares or whatever can give us any information on what's going on. The more we know the better."

"I still don't understand how this will help," I grumbled, uncurling from her car and gasping when the chill air smacked me like a fist in the gut. "Crappity crap cakes, its freezing."

"Also, please don't talk, Charlie." Ignoring my shivering, Tia looked at me pointedly over the top of the car. "Just bat your eyelashes, giggle, and act dumb, okay? If you say one more thing that makes you sound like a two-year-old, I might just kill you myself."

"You know what?" Frustrated, I was about to tell her to go in the club on her own, but that was all I managed to get out.

I took one step in the horrible high heels she made me wear and my ankle quit on me. My left foot twisted painfully to the side and gravity pulled me sideways to the unforgiving ground. My arms shot to the sides in a futile attempt to keep me standing, but the gravel greeted me anyway. Pebbles dug into the skin of my bare thighs and I landed with a grunt when the air was pushed from my lungs. I could still hear Tia muttering profanities that made my face burn through the white noise in my ears.

"Okay, change of plans," the human informed me while her and Glenda took hold of one arm each and yanked me back on my feet. "You don't talk, and no need to bat any eyelashes or giggle, but you must stay standing. Can you do that?"

"I really want to zap you right now," I hissed under my breath. "Can I zap her?" Glenda was already shaking her head no before I finished the question.

"Keep your back straight and your shoulders pulled back. Then all you have to do is put one foot in front of the other. Make sure you lock your knee on the leg that is carrying the weight at the time and you'll be golden." Fixing the wig on my head, Tia was firing directions at me faster than I could track them.

The High Priestess

Keeping the comments to myself, I watched in fascination as Glenda nodded and repeated everything Tia was saying under her breath as if she was trying to memorize it. That was when I realized I'd rather be in that scary world dealing with monsters from nightmares than learning how to be a human woman. Even if it was in disguise. A yelp was torn from my lips when Tia slapped my tush.

"Let's go," the human barked before marching ahead with Glenda trailing behind her.

I expected for us to wait at the end of the long line, hopefully long enough to not get inside at all. Unfortunately for me, Tia bypassed the angry humans, and smiling seductively at the two gorilla=chested bouncers got us in before I was mentally ready to enter the club. I knew something was going to go wrong as soon as the door closed behind me with a bang. The air was charged with anticipation. It was as if the lined bricks that formed the building rejoiced at having us in its gaping mouth.

Tingles started forming at my fingertips, and I rushed to catch up with the two women, high heels be damned. The bass of the music vibrated in my chest, and that still wasn't as hard as the thundering of my heart. My whole being was on alert, and that freaked the hell out of me. I hadn't felt like this, not even when I sulked around the clan mansion in the middle of the night, and there were killers lurking in the shadows there. I was hot on Glenda's heels when we reached the dance floor, and when my eyes adjusted to the pulsing lights, I understood my reaction. My gaze zeroed in on him like a moth to a flame.

Nigel the dumbnut was there.

Grinding my teeth, I waited until we reached the bar before getting my friends' attention and pointing our problem out by tilting my chin in his direction. Glenda's eyes widened, but Tia didn't bat an eyelash. Leaning over the bar, she waved at the bartender and ordered us drinks.

"Cheers." Tia grinned, but her eyes were too somber to match the cheery sound of her voice.

Squeezing the beer bottle the same way I wanted to strangle the bloodsucker, I clinked it off theirs while still keeping track of Nigel out of the corner of my eye. That was why we should've stayed in front of the hotel instead of playing dress up. We could've seen when he left and with whom. And because we took the time so I could pretend I was something I wasn't, we had probably missed something important.

"He is headed this way," Glenda hissed in my ear and stiffened next to me.

Before I could react, Tia grabbed the seer by the hand and dragged her to the dance floor, leaving me all alone at the bar. I glared daggers at her when she grinned at me over her shoulder, but that didn't help me at all. I felt his nearness before his scent filled my nostrils, and then it drowned any other smell in the vast space. The problem I had was not Nigel himself, per se.

Okay, it was him to a point.

The sour taste in my mouth, however, was because I wasn't sure if he was aware of the possibility of Selena being a host to a monster and turning a blind eye for his own gain. Or maybe he knew that she was a host for sure, and if he did, he had decided not to warn me, that was for sure. Either way, I had drawn the short stick so he could get what he wanted. It wasn't sitting well with me at all. So I stared at the back of his head when he waved his empty glass at the bartender and asked for a refill.

"If I didn't know better, I'd say you are following me Ms. Jansen." He spoke before turning to face me, but it did

The High Priestess

the trick to jolt me right out of my murderous thoughts. "And you wanted to make sure I didn't recognize you."

"How did you know it was me?" I knew this wouldn't work, and I was going to kill Tia for making me dress like an idiot.

"The disguise would've worked." His gray eyes rolled over me from head to toe leaving goosebumps in their wake. "If your power was not battering my defenses like a deranged mule in heat."

I jerked like he had just slapped me.

"You son of a biscuit eater ..."

"Now, now darling." Yanking me to his side, his fingers crushed the bone of my upper arm when I tried to get away. "Let's not attract attention, stop struggling and lean closer to me." When my eyebrows crawled to my hairline when he rolled his eyes at me. "You want everyone to think you are human. It's what a human woman will do around me."

Begrudgingly, I stopped tugging my arm from his hold and tentatively leaned on his side. "I thought my powers were battering defenses like a mule in heat."

"I said it was battering mine, Ms. Jansen." The damn dimple popped into existence on his cheek, and my fingers twitched from the need to slap the smirk off his face. "I didn't say a word about anyone else seeing through your disguise. You should wear clothing like this more often." His smoldering gaze had me dazed for a moment before the offhanded comment registered in my brain.

My elbow dug into his ribs, and he grunted in pain.

"Next time you say something dimwitted like that I will fry your family jewels." Grinning like a fiend, I batted my eyelashes at him. "Maybe then you can find a different metaphor for my magic instead of a mule in heat."

"Something is different about you, Charlie." When his

chuckling ended and he was done rubbing his ribs, Nigel narrowed his eyes on me. "What have you been up to since I last saw you?"

"None of your business. You're not my mother." Not wanting to accidently slip about my trip through the gate, I changed the subject. "Where is your watch dog? I didn't see her around."

"I'm assuming you are asking about Selena?" His arm snaked around me, and I stiffened when his hand started gliding up and down my back, low enough that I could feel his pinky finger brushing my tailbone with each stroke.

"How many watch dogs do you have?" Pretending I didn't notice, I was proud of the even tone of my voice.

"She is entertaining your uncle's hound." Searching my face, he kept petting me like we were lovers, which irked me to no end. "I needed time away and to think, so here I am."

"And you picked the perfect place for thinking: The Cauldron." Snorting, I grimaced at the blunt lie.

His lips twitched at the corners, and I hated myself for noticing.

"I went to think at the docks on Elizabet River." His knowing smirk brought heat to my cheeks. "I came to The Cauldron for the same reason you are here."

"Which is?" Cocking an eyebrow, I squirmed when his hand stayed at the top of my butt for too long.

A wicked smile stretched his face. "Information, Ms. Jansen. What else?"

"Information on what?" I asked after the bartender brought his drink, took the bill to charge him, and almost kissed his hand when Nigel didn't want change. One hundred bucks for one drink.

Must be nice to be Nigel Thatcher.

"I am not yet sure." A line formed between his perfectly

shaped eyebrows. At least his maddening, roaming hand dropped away from my butt so I could think.

A familiar figure caught my attention over the bloodsuckers shoulder, and without giving myself time to overthink my actions, I kicked off the high heels and picked them up with my fingertips. Nigel's eyebrow lifted in question, and I only grinned at him.

"The time has come for sharing of information part of the night." Sidestepping away from his body with great effort was a bad idea.

The demon I'd chased not long ago to get info on how to find Nigel saw me the second I moved away from the bloodsucker. His face scrunched in confusion because he didn't recognize me with my wig and contacts, but his survival instinct did not betray him. Spinning on his heel, he bolted for the front doors, flinging people to the side like they were bowling balls. I darted after him, my bare feet sliding on the smooth floor. Nigel was right behind me.

"What do you think you are doing?" I hissed at him over my shoulder.

"Ms. Jansen," the son of a cracked nut chided. "You don't think I would miss this for anything in this world, do you?"

"Mother fudging, crappity titty chomper."

Regardless of my frustration, a smile lifted the corners of my lips when I heard him chuckle.

"You are a dumbnut, Charlie," I muttered under my breath.

This time he laughed.

Chapter Eight

I barreled through the front doors of the club like a bull on steroids, my long strides making my barely-there dress to bunch at the tops of my thighs. The bite in the air was teasing my nether regions, and that reminded me that I was probably flashing my tush at the vampire still hot on my heels. His intent gaze was like a physical touch burning the back of my head, but if I wanted to catch the slippery dimwit running like his life depended on it, then I didn't have time to worry about Nigel.

Why was he even following me?

It spoke volumes as to how much people owning and working at The Cauldron cared what happened to the people who frequented there, especially when the two gorillas standing guard at the front doors didn't even flinch when I zoomed past them. It almost made me think that people dashing through the doors like their butts are on fire was an every-night occurrence. The humans, mostly the guys with leering gazes, were not so indifferent to my

The High Priestess

barely-covered self, and the few cat calls and whistles had my face so hot I could hardly stand it. The ferocious snarl coming from behind me silenced them, though it triggered my own fight or fright instincts. The son of a biscuit eater could've had the demon pinned by now if he'd used his speed, but for whatever reason he was lingering behind me like some creepy crawler while I did all the work.

"There," Nigel snapped, his hand shooting over my shoulder to point at the demon taking the corner around the building.

A sense of déjà vu hit me like a slap to the cheek as I watched the dimwit take the same route as the last time I'd chased him when I'd been looking for information so I could find Nigel. Even the salty tang in the air was the same, which only left my choice of clothing and the unpleasant tug of the wig where the bobby pins stabbed my skull as a reminder that this was just how my life was. Chasing idiots across streets and through parking lots of Norfolk was par for the course with me.

I took the turn wide at the corner, my bare feet scraping over sharp pebbles that shredded my skin. The few lampposts that used to cast a dim yellow glow over the parked cars struggled to pierce the foggy night air, turning the open space into some zombie movie set ready for action. Unlike last time, the parking lot was packed with cars, and it forced me to zigzag through them. I kept my eyes trained on the hardly-visible head bobbing ahead of me while the idiot ran. Also different was the fact that I was way too aware of the bloodsucker's nearness, his power teasing my senses and poking at mine like a pestering fly I couldn't shake off.

The demon was gaining ground while I was too preoccupied with Nigel and the reason he was behind me in the first place, the silhouette of his body barely noticeable through the fog and the dark shadows of the parking lot. Worried that I might lose him and my chance to find out what he knew about the monster that sneaked out through the gate, I glanced at my hand where I was still clutching the heels in a white-knuckled grip. The loss of focus cost me. I slammed my hip into the back of a sports car, the sharp edge of its taillight sending excruciating pain shooting through my lower body. My body spun in a half circle, the balls of my feet scraping painfully over the cement. Gravity tried to drag me down, but strong hands gripped my upper arms and yanked me straight up until my legs were dangling like loose threads in the air.

"What ..." Gasping, I stumbled slightly when Nigel deposited me back on the ground without missing a beat.

"Keep up, Ms. Jansen." His deep voice was full of amusement, while I couldn't stop grinding my teeth and staring daggers at the back of his head after he jogged past me.

He was jogging for Pete's sake, while I was huffing and puffing like I was trying to bring a brick house down.

At least he is no longer staring at your bare ass, dumnut. The voice in my head reminded me to count my blessings.

My eyes darted to the last place I saw the demons head sticking out between the cars and barely saw it disappearing behind a large SUV. Instead of following the bloodsucker, I sprinted left and ran parallel with him in hopes to see him when he cleared the vehicle. My fingers twitched where I held the shoes just as he popped out from in front of the SUV. Without thinking, I transferred one shoe into my free hand, cocking the other arm back and releasing the glossy black high-heel through the air like it was a throwing star. It spun fast, flying over two rows of cars before connecting with the side of his head with a tooth-shattering thud.

Thump!

Flinching at the sound, my shoulders lifted all the way to my ears when the demon dropped like a sack of potatoes and disappeared from sight. Skidding to a stop, I panted to catch my breath while I stared wide-eyed at the last place I saw his head. Honestly, I was too afraid to move. Did I just kill the poor shmuck? I wasn't even aware that I could throw that far or that I had such accuracy in nailing a faraway moving target. A low whistle not far from me snapped my head in that direction, the drumming of the heartbeat in my throat forcing short puffs of air to pass through my lips until they formed faint clouds in front of my face.

"I am impressed, Ms. Jansen." Nigel clapped slowly as he sauntered to where I was standing.

"Did I kill him?" I gawked dumbly at the smirking bloodsucker.

"That would be quite unfortunate, I would think." His British accent was more prominent as he looked me up and down, his eyes lingering a little too long for my comfort around my hips. "Dead men cannot talk. Isn't that why we are running like idiots after him? You need information?"

I blinked at him.

"Shall we?" Like some knight at a ball and not a dimwit chasing demons with me in a parking lot, he flung his arm in front of me with flourish so I could walk ahead of him. "Demons have hard skulls, so I'm most certain he is only dazed. Let us intercept him before he comes around."

"Your sense of compassion is astounding," I grumbled dryly, but I hurried ahead of him to make sure I really didn't kill the demon.

I shrugged my neck into my shoulders when I rounded

the car and saw the person sprawled on the ground unmoving. The shoe I used as a weapon was flipped over next to his arm so that the thin heel was pointing up at me accusingly. Frozen in the spot I stood, my gaze darted from the demon to Nigel, who I found leaning his hip on the hood of the car with his arms folded across his chest as if he was bored. My lips parted so I could ask the bloodsucker if the guy was dead, because not even I could miss the dark liquid trickling from his temple and matting his hair. The vampire's nose didn't miss it either, and he was at least a mile away, I was sure.

A groan silenced my words.

"You are alive." Relief flooded me like a tsunami and my knees buckled until I dropped next to the demon. "Are you okay? I mean, you're bleeding but ... are you okay?"

Ignoring the snorting coming from the bloodsucker, my undecided hands hovered over the demon. My natural reaction was to touch him so I could assure myself that he was indeed alive, but my inclinations of staying away from physical contact were screaming at me that it was a stupid idea to touch him. The poor thing was groaning and writhing on the ground, clutching the side of his head while blinking his dazed eyes rapidly. One of my hands lowered on its own to reach for his shoulder just as his gaze cleared and he snapped it at my face.

"Don't kill me, clipper." His frightened shout made me jump.

"What? No." Shock was replaced by confusion that pulled my eyebrows down, but I didn't miss his trembling. He was scared. Terrified even. "I'm not killing you. I am making sure you are alive."

"After she lobbed you with a stiletto sharp enough to stab you in the eye and exit at the back of your head." The ever-helpful bloodsucker pointed out, and his tone was so casual I almost believed we were all just standing around hanging out. "I apologize for the intrusion, Ms. Jansen. Go on, you were doing marvelously." He waved me on when I glared at him, which left my mouth hanging open.

"Oh shit!" When the demon's eyes landed on Nigel, the demon scrambled on the ground like a turtle trying to right itself after landing on its back. "I did what you asked. The clipper can tell you I gave her the information. Please don't kill me."

Frowning, I looked from the demon to Nigel and back, not missing the gloating smirk on the vampire's face. What in the world was he talking about? Realization came in the form of a meteor dropping on top of my head. The déjà vu feeling smacked into me even harder this time, and I envisioned chasing the demon in this very parking lot, and then my mind fell to when he told me that Nigel was visiting Black Cat in search of magical objects, which sent me right in Selena's clutches. That was the trigger, the thing that had brought me out tonight, and the same thing that had me stuck bonded to the Necronomicon and searching for a thing of nightmares.

The arrogant tilt of Nigel's mouth confirmed it.

"You fudging mother trucking titty chomper!" Hissing in outrage, I wiggled to my feet, tugging on my damn dress to cover my tush. "You set me up."

"I thought we already covered that conclusion, Ms. Jansen." The bloodsucker shrugged unapologetically, and the trembling demon only gaped at both of us while on his knees on the ground. "I would not be who I am if I didn't stay one step ahead at all times."

It disturbed me to no end that Nigel not only set me up from day one, but he also knew way more about me than any other person alive. For him to plant information, he must've known where I'd go looking for it, and in my world that was a very dangerous thing. Being shunned by every one of my kind had made me predictable, and predictable for an Assassin Mage was a one-way ticket to hell. Hearing this little tidbit brought a little clarity, too. I was an easy target, and sadly, I lived my life thinking I was smarter than the rest of my clan.

Nigel's voice dragged me out of my sullen thoughts. "I am not here for you," he told the demon in a bored tone. "The lady wants to ask you a question. I would answer her truthfully if I were you."

The light from the lamppost closest to us was casting an angelic golden light over his perfect face, which made his cheekbones appear sharper and showcased his dimple that kept blinking at me when he smiled. That should've put me at ease, but Nigel Thatcher smiling the way he was at that moment looked as innocent as dunking your bleeding leg inside a pool while a hungry crocodile waited in the depths. The demon eagerly turned his attention to me, seeming much more willing to share what he knew than any other time I'd chased him around. I wanted to scream or punch something for getting myself involved in all this, but given the extenuating circumstances I was in, my shoulders dropped as I turned to the informant. I'd deal with the son of a cracked nut later.

"What do you know of a nightmare creature looking for a host in our world?" the demon blanched the second I started talking, and even in the darkness I could see stark red blood vessels popping through the whites of his eyes.

That got Nigel's attention as well.

The bloodsucker straightened and his full attention fell on my face, but I did everything possible to ignore him. He

The High Priestess

would have questions. Lots of them when this was over, but I couldn't worry about that now. From what that creature had told me, time was of the essence and I'd wasted enough of it lurking in front of the vampire's hotel. I needed something, anything really, to point me in the right direction before it was too late. As if to remind me how messed up my life was, the whispers in the back of my mind grew louder.

"You are in way over your head, clipper." There was no mistaking the fear in the demon's voice. Goosebumps covered my arms, seeing his horror silencing the noise in my head. "Not even *I* am stupid enough to tell you anything about it. If I had any information, which I don't." Shuffling on his knees, he turned to face Nigel. "You can kill me, Blade. I know nothing."

The demon was off the cement with his feet hanging uselessly before I had time to blink. Nigel was holding him a foot off the ground by his neck like the shmuck weighed as much as a feather. His eyes bulged while he clawed at the vampire's wrist, and the gurgling sounds he was making were much too loud in the quiet of the parking lot.

"Put him down." Snapping at the bloodsucker, I tugged on his free arm. "He knows something, but he can't tell us if you kill him."

"You think?" Unperturbed, Nigel turned to face me while still dangling the demon in the air. The cruel glint in his gray eyes sent a shiver up my spine, reminding me that he was not a harmless puppy I was trying to train. The predator was out in full force, and my magic reacted to that, swimming to the surface. My fingers twitched from the sensation, and the back of my head went numb.

Nigel narrowed his eyes on me.

"Will you put him down ... please." I squeezed that last part through my clenched teeth.

"Well I'll be damned. You do have manners Ms. Jansen." The demon plopped on the ground like a fish out of water, coughing and wheezing when Nigel released him.

"Where can I find the host?" Ignoring the asphole who was smirking at me, I tried to take advantage of the situation. Releasing both my swords, I pointed the tip of one at the demons throat until he stopped his flailing. "Speak, before I bleed you out slowly."

"I was dead the moment he found me and told me I must give you the information when you seek me out," the demon rasped, looking up at me with flat, empty eyes. "I just hope to live long enough to see that creature feast on your bone marrow, clipper. Dying will be worth it then."

His head snapped to the side when Nigel's fist connected to it. The demon's body started listing to the side, but the bloodsucker yanked him back and fisted his shirt hard enough that the fabric ripped at the seams.

"Answer the question and keep your comments to yourself. There are many ways for you to suffer while still breathing," Nigel snarled in his face.

"You want to find the host?" The demon's voice shook and spittle flew from his lips. "Look at your own house and those in it. I hope it prolongs your deaths."

I watched in horror when his fingers sharpened into talons, the black pointy tips sinking into his own chest. He laughed a crazed, unhinged sound as his hand twisted and he ripped it out with his still beating heart in his palm. Numb from shock, I watched his eyes roll to the back of his head before the organ plopped to the ground with a wet, squelching sound. And then his body went limp. There was no time to recover from the terrifying picture, not before the demon's body started drying out. It turned into a husk first, and then it was ash. Cold wind whipped my hair around, blowing the ashes and scattering them across the grime-covered ground.

"There you are."

My startled gaze locked with Nigel's when a familiar woman's voice spoke from across the dimly-lit parking lot.

Chapter Nine

My squeaked protests were swallowed by a deep, amused chuckle when Nigel yanked me to his chest and tucked his face into the crook my neck. One arm was curled around my waist to keep me pinned to his hard body, his other hand tangled in my red wig while his strong fingers controlled my head. He turned slowly, taking me with him so he could face the woman standing on the other side of the parked car. Seemingly reluctant, he lifted his head to peer over my shoulder at her, an annoyed bite entering his words.

"What seems to be so important for you to seek me out, Selena?" the bloodsucker drawled, and it dawned on me that his actions were more to hide my identity from her than Nigel being a typical dimwit and doing things just to get a reaction from me. Playing along, I allowed him to move me around, loosely making my whole weight settle in his arms.

I held my breath.

"A redhead? How typically male of you, Sire." Selena snorted but didn't approach us, thank the fates. "Since when do you hunt your own food?"

"Since the lot of you bore me out of my brains," he deadpanned, and I had to bite hard on my lip so I could hold back the bark of laughter threating to escape me. "Well? Out with it." His British accent thickened so much it made me wonder just how hard he tried to cover it up when speaking to me.

"We have a problem." The witch—if she even was a witch, but I had no idea what else to call her—huffed in irritation. "The mages just became a major pain in our ass."

Nigel blinked lazily at her.

His face was so close to mine that his long lashes tickled my cheekbone as I stared at him from the corner of my eye. My eyeballs hurt because I had to strain them so much to look at him, but I had to see his expression to be able to judge the situation. I was very grateful that the shock of seeing the demon kill himself dissipated my swords into nothing. It would've been very difficult to pull off being one of Nigel's blood banks with swords clutched in my hands.

"That old fool is mobilizing the entire Jansen clan to search for the girl. It went as far as him seeking assistance from the rest of the assassin clans." Anger made Selena spit the words full of venom.

I stiffened.

My uncle cared that much about me that he recruited the rest of the clans to search for me? He wouldn't be caught dead talking to the rest of the clan leaders outside of the mage's guild meetings. Gobsmacked, I racked my brain to figure out what that meant. Firstly, I thought he would be relieved that I was gone and he no longer had to deal with my useless self and my stupidities, as he liked to call them. Secondly, didn't he tell me to run himself? And most importantly, he knew about my friendship with Tia. Why weren't killers crawling all over her apartment building waiting on their chance to snatch me? What in the world was going on here? Either Selena was lying and making crapcakes as an excuse to explain why she followed Nigel here, or ...

Or my uncle was warning me by keeping my human friend secret before he started the hunt for real.

The blood curdled in my veins.

The whispers in my mind perked up at my fear.

"This concerns me how, exactly?" The bloodsucker's bored tone pulled me out from my panic. Was he serious right now?

"She has the book." There was no room left for doubt in her clipped tone. "Nothing will convince me otherwise. We find the girl and we find the Necronomicon." The heels of her shoes tapped the cement while she paced, the sound projecting her agitation loud and clear. Still, she didn't come closer to Nigel, which was puzzling to say the least, especially if she was indeed the host for Nira.

And I thought the elder wood wand was my biggest problem when it came to Selena.

Karma had struck again.

"Then why are you here, Selena?" Nigel's question startled both me and the witch since she abruptly stopped. I jerked back to see his face better.

"That hotel is no longer safe for you." Changing tactics, she switched from being pissed off to sounding worried and reasonable. Even I could tell she was trying to play him. "Mages are crawling all over the floors like cockroaches. We need you to move to a safer place."

"Shall I start calling hotels or real estate agents at this ungodly hour so I can have a roof over my head come morning?" The mild, soft tone of his voice was the scariest thing I'd heard to date, including listening to Ulthar talk in a different realm. It promised pain and suffering, and my skin turned clammy from the sound as I shivered in his arms.

"That's my job." Selena sounded pouty and put out as she pushed the words out slowly. "I just wanted you to be aware of what is happening. That is why I searched for you." There was not a trace of the sass she displayed the first time she spoke. Not that I blamed her. I was barely keeping my bladder from giving up on me.

"I have been informed. Leave." The dismissal felt like a slap to my own ears, and I couldn't help but brace for whatever tantrum Selena was going to throw his way.

All my thoughts evaporated into mist when the vampire tugged my head to the side, bearing my neck. When his full lips closed over my jugular, I almost jumped away, but his fangs never sank into my skin. Somewhere in the back of my mind I logically understood that it was another way of telling the witch to get lost, and that definitely worked in my favor, but all that got lost in translation when my hormones kicked into overdrive and forced my body to react like it was the Fourth of July and they were the main fireworks show for the night. Every nerve I possessed came to life, buzzing under my skin as if I had plunged my fingers inside a power socket. Mortified, I listened to the low, husky moan pass my lips while my back arched until I was pressing my hard-as-rocks nipples to his chest. Nigel was wearing a faded t-shirt that molded to his body like a symbiont creature feeding off his muscular frame. There was no way he didn't feel the stiff peaks stabbing at him like they were trying to get his attention.

The arm wrapped around my waist stiffened, the muscles of his forearm turning into granite while his fingers tightened painfully where he clutched the wig and my hair simultaneously. In the background, the sound of footsteps faded as Selena stalked off to plot my early death, no doubt. I couldn't even use being blasted with a magic wand to get out of the situation, although it sounded like a good way to go and be saved from facing Nigel. His lips glided further up my neck tentatively as if judging my reaction, and my treacherous body pressed closer to his chest on its own.

"Is she gone?" I hated the fact that I sounded breathy, but I had to say something to break the silence and his unnerving attention to every twitch I made. Nigel said nothing, but his head lifted and he removed those stupidly soft lips from my pebbled skin. After that, I felt more than saw him staring at my face.

"Well?" I hissed at him.

"Not yet." He spoke so low that I mostly understood his words by the vibration they made in his chest.

Nigel was a manipulative son of a biscuit eater, and he never did anything just because. Every move, hell, every breath he took and didn't need to take was calculated to serve him and his interests to the best of its ability. I wasn't deluding myself that Nigel the mother fudging Thatcher was hitting on me, or somehow developed a heart and I, in all my graceless glory, affected him. There was an angle he was chasing. I just couldn't see it at the moment. Well, an angle other than the cursed book, but that one was as clear as the midday sun to me from day one. I almost jumped out of my skin when the tip of his nose grazed the column of my throat and he sniffed me.

It wasn't even an inconspicuous whiff like people do in passing occasionally if a scent teases their senses. Oh, no. Not Nigel Thatcher. He took his sweet freaking time and

The High Priestess

inhaled slowly, savoring it until my lower belly fluttered from wings of imaginary butterflies and I had to press my thighs together so I didn't push him on the ground and make a moron out of myself by molesting him. To snap my brain out of the crazy thoughts involving the bloodsucker on the ground and me tearing his clothes off, I strained to hear how far Selena was in her retreat. I even reached out cautiously with my magic to test the area for any supernatural who might be standing around.

Deathly silence met my ears.

Apart from Nigel and those inside the Cauldron, there was no one else nearby. Not even across the street from the club, which told me Selena must've driven off or took a cab to wherever she was going next. Meaning that the bloodsucker was making a mockery of having me at his mercy. Those damn fangs were closer to my neck than they had any right to be, and there I was, hanging limply in his arms like an idiot. The bottom part of my tush felt frozen from the cold air thanks to the damn dress that was almost bunched up at my hips again. I was going to strangle Tia next time I saw her. The anger I felt toward Nigel spread to my human friend too, and before I knew it my fingers were tingling from my magic. Slowly, so he didn't notice what I was planning to do, I placed both palms at the center of Nigel's chest, moving my fingers gently as if I was petting him. Goosebumps covered my arms from the hungry growl that vibrated deep in his chest. His lips closed over my skin again, and this time his tongue joined the party. My brain was short-circuiting. My knees shook, too, but luckily logic prevailed.

I zapped him.

Not a slight warning zap either. Like a woman

possessed, I slammed my magic at the center of his chest hard enough to fling him off me and send him slamming into a car a few rows down. The front door of the vehicle dented, leaving a human shaped outline on it. The window shattered next, and glass rained over Nigel's head. When the alarm shrieked, all four lights blinked rapidly, their brightness enough to make me feel dizzy. Somehow I stayed planted to the spot with my hands firmly placed on my hips, glaring down at the son of a cracked nut.

He laughed.

The gull! Fury had me vibrating, and the damn alarm was giving me a pounding headache behind my eyes that was making it hard to think. Lifting a hand, I sent a rope of bright red magic sailing over the bloodsucker's head, hitting the car dashboard through the broken window and frying it to smithereens. The silence that followed was only disturbed by a few sputters from the car as it spat and coughed before completely dying off. That was when I noticed that the laughter had died down, too. My gaze snapped to Nigel's face and my heart skipped a beat.

"An impressive demonstration of power, Ms. Jansen." Pushing off the ground with one hand, he straightened and shook the broken glass from his hair by running his fingers through it. The whole time, he never took his gray eyes off me. "How else have you improved since the last time we had a chat like this?"

"I'm exactly the same as I was the day you chased me out of your hotel room so Selena didn't see I was there." Sticking to the truth as much as possible because he would be able to tell that I was lying, I turned the accusations at him. "Wanna tell me what that was all about? I thought the witch was your underling, oh mighty Sire. It looked to me like she was chastising you as if she was your mother a few minutes ago."

Narrowing his eyes, he watched me standing unnaturally still for long enough I almost started fidgeting. "Where is the book, Charlie?"

"Oh, so now I'm Charlie, am I?" I snorted ungracefully, which earned me a quirk of his lips, but it didn't last long at all. "Answer the question, Margie." My fingers twitched from my need to remove the smirk off his handsome face.

The wig was itchy on my head, so while I waited for him to speak, I ripped it from my head. A contented sigh sprang from me when the damn thing was finally off. Picking out the bobby pins, I speared my fingers through my poor hair and groaned in pleasure as my chipped nails scraped over my scalp. That was when I noticed Nigel was watching me with so much intensity it made my face burn hot. My hand dropped limply to my side.

"Well? Why are you hiding me from Selena?" Stabbing a finger at his face, I squinted at him. "I know you have tons of questions, but you'll be getting squat for answers unless you learn to share. Sharing is caring, Margie, so you better start talking or I'll leave."

"There is something off with her." I almost gasped when he spoke. I really wasn't expecting to get an answer. "I can't figure out what it is, but she ... she doesn't smell right." The confusion on his face would've been almost endearing if I didn't know who Nigel Thatcher was.

"Oh, I get it." I clicked my fingers before grinning at him. "You go around sniffing everyone like a security dog at the airport." Tilting my head to the side, I offered him a thoughtful look and tapped a forefinger on my chin. "Do you sniff the crotch, too? I'm asking so I can be ready to fend you off if you try, that's all."

The hunger burning in his gaze made me gulp audibly. Me and my big mouth. I had to go there, didn't I?

"There she is." Tia's shout made my eyes squeeze shut, but not before I saw the smug smile stretching Nigel's lips.

The night couldn't get any worse.

I wanted to slap myself as soon as the thought formed in my head.

Chapter Ten

I found myself squished in the back seat of Tia's car with Nigel, while the human and Glenda chatted cheerfully in the front. Not wanting to make a scene or throw a tantrum like a two-year-old, I clamped my mouth shut when Tia informed me all we were going back to her apartment. With the Necronomicon hidden in the same place, I had no idea what she was thinking inviting the bloodsucker to come along, but it wasn't like I could tell her that with him standing so close we would've kissed if I turned my head to face him. So, I stewed in the car, while he gloated and pretended to look out the window while keeping track of my every move from the corner of his eye.

"So, Nigel," Tia chirped, batting her eyelashes at the bloodsucker in her rearview mirror. "What can you tell us about this Selena chick?"

My eyes bulged and almost popped out of my skull.

"Tia!" I hissed at her, praying my heart would not give up on me. I knew Nigel could hear its frantic stuttering, but I couldn't care less. The human had lost her mind and was about to get us all killed. "What the hell is the matter with you."

"Oh." Instead of looking scared or even ashamed, she giggled. I couldn't do anything but gape at her as if she was a stranger I knew nothing about. "We forgot to tell you, sorry. Well, I'm not really sorry because it happened in the bathroom at the club while you were busy doing whatever you were doing outside with hottie." Her wink only made me want to throttle her more. "Anyway, Glenda had her thing. You know, when she zones out and goes all zombie-like? That. And now we know that hottie here has an important part to play in protecting you. Being the good sidekick I am, I figured we'll cut through the chase so all of us can get on the same page sooner rather than later. And here we are, on our way home to make a solid plan. You're welcome, by the way. Both of you."

"It's called a vision, and I'm not a zombie," Glenda mumbled, her body shrinking into the passenger seat as if she was trying to mold with it and disappear.

Nigel looked thoughtful as he stared at the back of Tia's head with a line puckering between his eyebrows.

"Why aren't you saying something?" I turned my anger on him because Tia was a lost cause. There was no reasoning with the crazy human and her fantasy of being a sidekick.

"What did you see in your vision?" Nigel addressed Glenda gently, which was very different than his aspholish attitude when talking to me.

"There is death looming over Charlie's shoulder waiting to catch her unawares. It wants control over the ..." she trailed off, taking a loud breath that seemed to come all the way from her toes, but we all knew what she didn't say. The book. It wanted control over the book. "In my vision, a

The High Priestess

blade sliced through the evil and saved her life. If the blade was not there at the right moment, not just her life will end, but all of ours will too. Evil will take over our world and all of us will die. Supernatural and human alike."

"And you got Nigel from this vision how exactly?" Tia took a sharp turn and skidded around the corner. Of course my butt slid across the seat, which plastered my body right up against the bloodsucker. He looked way too pleased with the situation, even as I shoved against him with both hands to get myself away.

"Don't you go by the name Blade most of the time?" It was Tia who asked the question, and she spoke to Nigel while doing a bang-up job of ignoring me. I regretted telling the two women everything the night when I bonded with the Necronomicon. They were using everything they could against me.

"It is known as my name by most, apart from a select few, yes," he answered politely, and his tone set my teeth on edge.

"Your select few are expanding to quite a few." Childish, I knew, but I couldn't help myself. I was irritated with the whole situation, and we were a couple of minutes away from the apartment.

"So it seems." His short reply had no anger in it, just mild wonder as if he was intrigued by the prospect of more people knowing his true identity.

Everyone had lost their marbles.

My mouth opened but I had no time to say anymore stupid things just to irritate the bloodsucker. A dark shadow ballooned in front of the car, and it forced Tia to yank hard on the steering wheel. Luckily, she managed to take a side street instead of slamming head-first into one of the tall buildings. The tires screeched over the asphalt, the back of the car fishtailing until she gained control again and crushed the gas pedal to the floor. My back pressed hard on the seat when we sped up, but the dense shadow was right on our heels. My heart drummed a staccato beat against my ribs while I craned my neck to see how close it was.

Nigel was twisted to the side too, looking through the back window with a narrowed gaze. A muscle jumping in his jaw was the only indication he was fuming. How dare whatever that thing was try to intercept Nigel Thatcher on his night out on the town. It should've made an appointment to check when it was convenient for the bloodsucker. My snort at that thought got his attention, but he looked at me like I was the one who had lost her mind. My fear was choking me, so I chose humor to relieve the tension threatening to rip my skin from my bones. If it bothered him, he was more than welcome to get the hell out of the car.

We all jolted when the shadow hit the back of the car with a hard thump. The back lights broke and sprinkled over the street, but it only made Tia press harder on the gas, driving so fast I was sure we would end up wrapped around one of the mermaid statues sprinkled on every corner of the city. It was a better outcome than that thing catching up to us, especially after the stench of melted metal and plastic reached my nostrils. Whatever it was made of was deadly enough to destroy a part of the care with just one touch.

I swallowed thickly.

"What do you think you are doing?" I screeched when Nigel pushed the door on his side open.

"She can't keep up. It'll eventually reach the same speed," Nigel explained calmly as if we were discussing the weather. "I'll go outside and try to get it to follow me."

"She's driving a hundred and forty miles an hour," I pointed out.

The High Priestess

"If I didn't know better, I'd say you were worried about me, Ms. Jansen." He repeated the same nonsense he was spewing that night in his hotel when he drilled me about The Magician.

Another bump jolted us, and the stench of the back of the car melting grew stronger. Glenda whimpered in the front, while Tia was rigid as she squeezed the steering wheel in a white-knuckled grip. The door that Nigel was holding slightly open almost ripped from his grasp, but he pulled it back enough that it didn't hinder the speed we were driving. Freezing air blasted through the gap, but it didn't help at all to stop my sweating. If I didn't think of something, the crazy bloodsucker was going to jump out of the car. I didn't like Nigel much, and I definitely didn't trust him, but I didn't want him to die. And my friends were going to die, too. Either from the thing chasing us or from a car crash.

The whispers made themselves known in the back of my mind.

With no other options left, I let them come louder, allowing them to overtake every other thought. My stiff muscles loosened, my body losing the frightened posture and turning more pliant so that I could flip around on my knees and face the shadow through the back window of the car. Nigel glanced at me before doing a double take and closing the door with a loud bang. The sound came from afar, but I felt his eyes on me. For a split second I wondered what he saw, but Tia's sharp intake of air told me I didn't want to know.

My skin felt too tight to contain me as the magic poured inside me and stretched it to bursting. I could sense it everywhere in this city, from the cracked bumpy roads to the brick walls of the buildings. It reached for me like an old friend and filled me to the point that I was almost high from it. An invisible wind lifted the strands of my hair until they floated around me as if I was standing underwater, and my hands burned with the need to blast the damn thing threatening our lives.

Nigel shifted as well, and before I could see what he was doing, he punched the back window hard enough to shatter it to tiny pieces. It sprayed the shadow racing after us, but the glass disappeared in it without a sound. It looked like a cloud of dark fog, nothing remarkably scary if it wasn't for the menacing energy pulsing from it in waves that blasted my senses. The short hairs at the back of my neck lifted in reaction to it, but the markings on my skin flared as if reminding me I didn't have to cower meekly. If this thing wanted me dead, I'd go down kicking and screaming, preferably taking it along with me.

"Charlie!" Nigel's shout told me that wasn't the first time he'd called my name. I turned my eyes away from the shadow and locked them on his face. "What do you need me to do?"

I blinked at him.

"I will not stand in your way, but I will not allow you to kill yourself, Ms. Jansen." The stubborn set in his jaw told me he wasn't going to drop it. "What are you planning to do?"

"Blast it with magic?" It was the only thing I could think of. It didn't have a body for me to fight, and I definitely didn't want to touch it so I'd melt like all the pieces of the car it had touched.

Nigel gave me a sharp nod of approval.

Ignoring the strange behavior of the bloodsucker, I looked back at the shadow. It was much closer now, almost touching the back of the car. Tia took another sharp turn and the tires screeched across the asphalt loud enough to hurt my ears. Glenda yelped when her head thumped on the window, her soft sobs stabbing me in the heart. She thought we were about to die. I did too, but at least I could try to fight it. Lifting both my palms in front of me, I gasped as two hands took hold of my waist when my body swayed in the moving vehicle. Nigel shuffled on his knees and braced himself behind me, pressing my back to his chest.

"Don't hold back," he murmured in my ear, his nearness sending butterflies through my stomach. "I'll hold you stable so you can focus on hitting your target."

It was an unprecedented show of trust to let a predator like Nigel at your back, but I didn't have time to think too hard about it. The magic flooding my system was about to split me open, so I focused on the shadow and sank further into Nigel's body. Coolness spread through my back everywhere our bodies touched, which only elevated the burn trying to consume me from the inside. The whispers were now hungry screams wanting to devour the shadow for daring to threaten our lives.

Spreading my fingers as wide as they could go, I released a blast of magic at the shadow. Bright electric blue burst from my palms like a torrent with the strength of a waterfall slamming into the rocks in the riverbed reaching to meet it. The light was so strong that I had to squeeze my eyes shut, but Nigel's pained grunt pulled my focus back where it needed to be. The magic kept pouring from my hands and drilling a hole at the center of the shadow. When the brightness slightly dimmed, I blinked a few times and held my breath, hoping I'd done enough damage to stop it. My heart paused before jumping into my throat and hitting the roof of my mouth.

It pierced the shadow, but it only split it into two of them that were writhing and gunning for us now. My arms were trembling, and Glenda's cries were ripping my heart to shreds. With great effort, I lifted my noddle-like arms and prayed to anyone who would listen to help me stay strong enough for another attack. I could hear Tia murmuring assurances to the seer, my human friend's voice shaking as she kept telling Glenda everything was going to be okay.

But it wasn't okay.

And it wasn't going to be if I couldn't handle another power surge like the one before. My body was protesting, and my heart was painfully thumping against my ribs. Every nerve ending felt like it was on fire, and my skin felt too hot to the touch. I wasn't sure about anything, but I knew for certain the amount of magic I expended the first time was not normal. We were born with it in our blood, but we could also die from it if given too much. Just like the one I pulled inside myself a few minutes ago. But what choice did I have?

A cool hand pressed into the center of my belly, pulling me into the body of the male behind me. His other hand joined it, the chilled touch of his skin taking away some of the heat. Nigel pressed the side of his face to mine, nuzzling it, his five o'clock shadow scraping my skin pleasantly. He tightened his hold on me and took a deep breath.

"You can do this, Charlie." I could tell there was more that he wanted to say, so I waited and blinked away the tears that were burning at the back of my eyes. "I knew where you were because I took your blood. I will always know where you are, but I can also feel that you can do this. Stop doubting yourself. Just let go and do what feels natural to your body. Leave everything else to me."

Dark spots danced at the corners of my eyes, and I knew exactly what he was asking me to do. If I pulled another torrent of magic into my body like I did before, I'd

The High Priestess

be unconscious when I released it at the shadow. Nigel, the most manipulative, most deadly vampire in the world was asking me to not just trust him with my own life, but also with the lives of my two friends. My only friends. The problem was, I had no other option unless I did nothing more and hoped we somehow survived this attack.

The car fishtailed when one of the shadows smacked it from the side.

Glenda screamed, and I closed my eyes as I clenched my fists.

I nodded once.

"Thank you." His soft words snapped my eyes open.

I didn't want to think, or to humanize Nigel Thatcher, so I yanked on the magic, dragging it into each one of my pores. Tears ran freely down my cheeks, and my bones ached. I could feel them cracking from the strength of the power filling me. The whispers were frantic now, and it sounded like they were shouting and arguing among themselves. I floated outside my own body and observed all of it from a distance.

A loud pop announced that one of the shadows had eaten through a back tire. The metal alloy scraped the pavement and sparks shot everywhere. Tia didn't slow down. No, she kept weaving through the streets of Norfolk. I swore the girl should've been a Formula One driver. No one was as determined as my human friend when she set her mind to something.

"Charlie, stop dragging your ass and kill those fucking things," the human yelled at me, and although I was in excruciating pain, I couldn't help but smile.

"Yes ma'am," I called back to her, and my spirit lifted when I heard Glenda snort a laugh through her tears.

"If anything happens to them, I will hunt you for eternity, Margie."

"I will protect them with my life. You have my word." The somber tone of Nigel's deep voice was good enough for me.

Throwing my hands in front of me, I released the control I tightly guarded when it came to my magic. I wasn't expecting it to have a recoil. Power like I'd never felt before exploded out of me, slamming both Nigel and me into the backs of the front seats. I heard Tia yell something and Glenda call out, but I ignored it all as I watched in horror as the lava-like magic ate through the shadows like an eraser gliding over a pencil drawing. It was progressively harder to breathe after that. The heat was suffocating me, but I had to turn my head to the side so I could lock eyes with Nigel. His gray eyes were wide as they stared at what I'd done, but it didn't take long for his gaze to flick to mine.

"Remember what you promised." I barely managed to push the words out without puking all over him. Bile burned the back of my throat, and my markings pulsed under my skin.

"I gave you my word," he answered, but his gaze searched mine for something I couldn't name.

"Good."

That was all I could say before all the strength left me in a whoosh and I went limp in his arms. Call me an idiot, but I could've sworn I heard him whisper, "I'll guard you with my life, too."

Idiotic, I knew. Nigel Thatcher didn't care about anyone but himself. It was a good thing I knew him as well as I did.

Chapter Eleven

I woke to a world of pain. Every single bone in my body hurt, including those I wasn't aware that I had. Holding myself still, I made sure not a single muscle twitched. I didn't want to send another ripple effect through me, otherwise I might be seeing stars bursting behind my closed eyelids. There was pain even in my hair follicles, and it held me prisoner on the bed I was occupying. The weight pressing one of my arms to the mattress would've been negligible, but I was too freaked out because I was probably being held hostage somewhere. That thought was the one that had me wiggling to figure out what was holding me down and how I could break out of it.

"She's coming around." I blinked up to see Tia looming over me with a pinched look on her face. "Thank fuck. You are awake! You scared the shit out of me. Don't you ever do that again, Charlie."

"Okayyy ..." I breathed warily because of the crazed look in her eyes, gingerly twisting my head to the side so I could see what was pinning me to the bed.

"Hey," Nigel murmured, leaning over the bed on his forearms as he eyed me like I was on the verge of losing it. "How do you feel?"

Shock rendered me mute as my eyes traveled from his face to where his hand was wrapped around my arm holding it for dear life. His grip wasn't necessarily painful, but it was firm enough that it made question if they thought I was going to try to escape. Newsflash: I could barely blink, so I wasn't going to be making a run for it anytime soon. Why was he clinging to me like a five-year-old at the doctor's office?

"Like I was hit by a truck, a semitrailer traveling at maximum speed at that." A groan ripped from my chest when I tried to shift my hips to get more comfortable, and then I started to remember why I felt like roadkill left on the side of a highway for a week in the middle of summer. "I'm assuming I got that thing since we are all alive. Where is Glenda?"

"I'm here, Charlie." The seer shuffled closer to the bed so I could finally see her pale face. "You saved us." Her smile was sad, and tears shimmered in her haunted gaze.

"What was that thing?" Uncomfortable with Glenda's usual hero worship every time I did something remotely nice for her, I turned to the vampire who shouldn't even be here. "Have you seen anything like it before?"

"No."

"That's it? Just no?" My face hurt when I glared at him. Did we have bones inside our eyebrows? Because it felt like I had bones there and they hurt like the dickens.

"Yes, Ms. Jansen. No, I haven't seen anything like it." The cunning glint returned to his gray orbs, but he didn't release my arm. His accent thickened, and his intense gaze made my heart beat faster. "Given the situation, we

The High Priestess

shouldn't be surprised. We will be dealing with many things in the near future that we've never seen before, I'm sure."

"What's that supposed to mean?" But I knew. My eyes flicked to the two women in the room, and the guilty look on their faces told me everything before Nigel uttered a word.

"I thought you were going to die." Tia jutted her chin out as if daring me to be angry at them for spilling everything to the bloodsucker. "I don't regret telling him. Not if it meant he could do something to help." When I stayed silent, she huffed and snatched Glenda's arm before stomping out of the room. "I'd do it again in a heartbeat, and you can be pissy as much as you want. I don't care."

"You bonded with the Necronomicon." The vampire waited until they were gone before he spoke. There was no accusation in his voice, but I still flinched back into the mattress. "It stands to reason that until you learn how to navigate your new life and connection, things will get ... how should I say it ... dicey."

"Right." The indignant snort coming from me made my chest hurt as I blinked up at the ceiling. "This is all your fault, you know? None of this would've happened if you'd just left me alone in the first place." When he said nothing, the silence seemed to stretch forever, at least until I cleared my throat. "Are you going to kill me now?"

"Why would I do that, Ms. Jansen?" The innocent curiosity in his tone did not fool me one bit.

"You wanted the Necronomicon for whatever use you have for it. Wasn't that what got us in this mess in the first place?"

"That is correct, but you see, I am a very adaptable creature. Otherwise, I wouldn't have been alive this long." My gaze locked on his while my heart drummed in my throat. His eyes focused on the throbbing vein in my neck, and I swallowed thickly. "I have heard the stories of the guardians, but I never expected to witness a myth come to life. You successfully managed to impress me at every turn, Ms. Jansen."

"It's very troubling to hear what you find impressive, Margie. The only thing I successfully managed to do was get myself in bullcrap up to my eyeballs." Hoping to buy more time so I could think about what this meant for me, I tried to tug my arm out of his grip. "Can I have my arm back, please?"

A line formed between his eyebrows when he looked down at his hand wrapped around my forearm. The confusion clouding his face told me that he wasn't aware he was holding onto me until I pointed it out. It was replaced fast by frustration, and then he glared at his limb as if it had offended him. A familiar unreadable mask settled over his features as he nonchalantly released me. After that, he straightened in his chair and slid it next to my bed, pretending like the last thirty seconds had never happened. If he wanted to act dumb, who was I to deny him?

"You were thrashing in your sleep, and the only thing calming you down was when I touched you." My look said he was a dimwit, but Nigel shrugged, though it was just a tiny twitch of one shoulder. "You can ask your friends; they wouldn't leave me alone with you. As if that would stop me if I wanted to hurt you."

"Have you met Tia?" Despite the gloomy situation, I couldn't help but smile.

"Are you ready to talk to me about the book?"

"Are you ready to tell me everything you know about it?" I countered, and he narrowed his eyes on me. "I didn't think so." Feeling awkward laying on a bed like an invalid

The High Priestess

while Nigel the son of a biscuit Thatcher was sitting next to it, I gritted my teeth and propped myself up so I could at least look him in the eye without staring up. "Trust works both ways, Margie."

"Indeed, it does," he murmured, and he was still squinting at me.

"And I thought I had trust issues." I barked a bitter laugh in his face. "You, buddy, are almost paranoid." It was the pot calling the cattle black, but whatever.

"They didn't have to tell me that you bonded with it." The sudden change of conversation gave me whiplash. "After seeing the display of power, it was as clear as a day, and it also confirmed the myth that the Necronomicon does have guardians. I suspected it to be true, but your existence confirms it."

Grateful for the lack of rainbow colors in Tia's guest bedroom, my eyes bounced from the tall dresser to the full-length mirror, finally landing on a small round table next to the window. I didn't know what to say to his comment because the idea of the magic I felt funneling through my body was making my head spin. The scariest thing about it was the fact that I never, not even for a second, stopped to question it. I had opened myself to the power I was familiar with, the one that had been coursing through my veins my entire life. I'd expected the temperamental magic to blast out of me in its usual blue or red flames. That was what it had always done. When the magic from all around me rushed to answer my call, I didn't second guess it. I took it all in like a parched man in the middle of the desert, soaking it up like a sponge.

I kept sucking it in, even when it felt my skin was going to rip to shreds.

Even when my heart kicked and stuttered like it was about to give up on me.

What does that say about me?

You are as power hungry as The Magician, a snide voice whispered in my mind, and the thought drenched me in cold sweat.

"I find it quite interesting that you see this as a horrible thing that happened to you, Ms. Jansen." Irked by the amusement in his voice, I clenched my jaw so I didn't tell him exactly what I thought about it. "As things are, you are the most powerful creature in the world. I fail to see how that can be a bad thing." My mouth dropped open and I gaped at him.

Throwing his head back, a deep belly laugh rolled off of Nigel while I was struggling to breathe.

"I don't want to be the most powerful creature anywhere." Pushing the words through numb lips, I concentrated on breathing so I didn't hyperventilate.

"That only makes you the perfect person to control such power." Another shrug, and then a smirk tugged at the corner of his mouth. "What am I going to do with you, Charlie?" All his humor evaporated as he watched me thoughtfully.

"Forget I exist, crawl back to whatever hole you crawled out of and leave me alone?" I piped in helpfully.

He grinned, the tips of his fangs peeking from under his upper lip.

"Something came through when The Magician had control of the book," I blurted out when my hormones poked their head out at Nigel's smile.

"What is that something that came through?" Leaning forward, he steepled his fingers in front of him, his forearms leaning on his thighs.

The High Priestess

"A creature that controls nightmares." Shivering when the memory of that place where I spoke to Ulthar popped in my mind, I crushed the bed covers in my hands to stop them from shaking. "A mate to the Lord of the Abyss, I was told. She is supposedly a priestess needing a host so she can stay in our world." Peeking at him from the corner of my eye, I waited for a reaction.

"That's why you were looking for the informant."

"The very useless informant, as it turned out." Bile burned at the back of my throat. "I can't believe he killed himself like that."

"Fear is a powerful thing, Ms. Jansen. It has no logic or reason." The silence stretched so long I thought we were done talking. I jumped a little when he spoke again. "You suspect Selena has something to do with it." It wasn't a question, so I didn't feel the need to answer him. "As I said, she has been acting strange lately."

"Strange how?" Pretending like it wasn't that important for me to hear it, I nestled even more into the pillows, although I admit I was dying to pepper him with a million questions. "She forgets to remind you when it's your nap time?"

His mouth twisted in a grimace at my jab. "She is very secretive, and unusually short tempered," Nigel mused.

"It could be the effect of the elder wood wand," I told him truthfully. "As far as I know, witches can't control a wand like that for a long time. It makes them go insane."

"She has been carrying it on her person often since we came to this city," he said, but I could tell it was more to himself than me.

Suspicion was eating a hole in my stomach, and my unseeing eyes darted from one object to another in the bedroom. If I wasn't feeling like death warn over, I would've been squirming being sealed into such close quarters with the bloodsucker. He wasn't good for my wellbeing, and that was something I'd learned the second his too-handsome face landed in my field of vision. So, why was I sitting here chatting with Nigel Thatcher like we were best buddies? Even with that in mind, I couldn't pass up the opportunity to keep drilling him when he was in such a chatty mood.

"The host does need to be a strong magic user." Throwing it as an offhanded comment, I stared at my fingers smoothing the bed cover. "Or so I was told."

"You think Selena is the host." There was no anger in him, and absolutely no frustration, so I pressed on.

"I can't guarantee it, but she does brandish the wand like it's not that big of a deal." Remembering my first encounter with the witch, I glanced at Nigel. "She changes her appearance easily, too."

"Glamor is not hard to do." He waved me off and my eyebrows kissed my hairline.

"For whom?"

"For a witch of her caliber, Ms. Jansen," he drawled as he leaned back in his chair. "I do not surround myself with useless individuals."

"Of course, how stupid of me to think you would even look at anyone if they didn't serve in some way, shape, or form that would further your agenda." My indignant snort resulted in a cocked eyebrow from the son of a cracked nut. "I mean, you are here playing a nursemaid, after all."

I should've been happy that he gave me a reminder of who he really was. A manipulative, cruel, and extremely ambitions son of a biscuit eater who only uses people until he no longer needs them, and then he discards them as if they were nothing. I was angry at myself for the ping in my chest at his admission. Was I honestly dumb enough to

The High Priestess

think for a second that there was redemption for the one person the whole supernatural world feared? It was obviously idiotic to argue with him without a sense of self preservation, but dumb I was not, and I needed to keep that thought at the front of my mind.

"Now that you know I didn't kick the bucket and your investment is safe, you are free to leave and spend your time with worthy individuals." Making a shooing motion with my hand, I closed my eyes and prayed that he would go away. "One more power outburst like the one I had before I passed out and I guarantee that the book will be free to bond with whoever it wants. You can come back then."

"You think I'm worried about the Necronomicon?"

"No, you just suddenly grew a conscience and care about my health now." My giggle sounded unhinged. "After you sent me to that hell so I could steal the cursed thing for you by threatening my life and the lives of everyone in my clan."

"And by default, making you the most powerful creature in the world." The bloodsucker reminded me of the one fact I'd been doing everything in my power to ignore.

"Which part of kicking the bucket didn't you get?" Unable to keep my eyes closed any longer, I glared at him. "You can think whatever you want, but I know the truth. I can't control it. It's too strong, and next time it's going to kill me."

"What is your plan to fix that little problem?" Nigel stood, and I breathed a sigh of relief. When he stretched his arms above his head and his t-shirt rode above the waistband of his jeans, I almost choked on that same sigh.

"Find a way to break the bond," I mumbled without thinking, and my lips were suddenly very dry.

"The answer to your problems is not breaking the bond,

Ms. Jansen. That's what an idiot would do." My gaze jerked from the bared skin on his abs to his face in time to see his arrogant smirk. Of course he had caught me drooling over him. Mother fudging dumbnut.

"Do share with the peasant the correct action we can take to fix the problem, Your Majesty," I purred, a condescending sneer oozing from my lips.

"You train." Unperturbed by my mocking, he tucked his hands behind his lower back, looking for all the world like a model acting as a professor in a commercial.

"I've trained to control my magic, unsuccessfully I might add, since I was five." All the energy drained from me all of a sudden, and it took all my fight too. My lids became so heavy I could hardly keep them open. "Unless you have a machine or a spell to freeze time so I can train for a century or two, I'm sorry to inform you, but I'm out of time."

And oddly enough, I was actually okay with it.

"That's because you were trained by bloody idiots." With his thick British accent, he dismissed the truth in my words. "It's a reflection of what they are lacking, not you, Ms. Jansen."

"Umm, okay." The words I spoke were slurred because my tongue felt way too thick in my mouth as I drifted in and out of sleep. I hoped he would get the hint and go away. "Too bad there is nothing you or I can do about it now."

"You better rest well. You will need it. I will see you tomorrow, Ms. Jansen." Nigel deluded himself that I was going to wait until he showed up here again. "There is always something that can be done."

"Umm …" His voice was coming from afar as I drifted further into oblivion, and I was happy that he was going away.

"I will train you."

The High Priestess

My eyes snapped open and I bolted upright into a sitting position on the bed, but I was too late. The door of the bedroom never opened, but the curtain moved and pulled my attention as the breeze coming from the open window billowed throughout the room.

"Mother fudge!"

Chapter Twelve

Two days passed with no sign of Nigel, nor with any progress on my part to find a lead that would help me discover who Nira's host was. Surprisingly, the whispers were silent for the most part, but that could've been because I was still feeing like a ninety-year-old grandma suffering from a severe case of arthritis. One good thing had come out of it, however, since I couldn't move around like a normal person and had to shuffle my feet or my muscles would spasm. I couldn't trip over my own feet. Just as I was thinking that, my pinky toe caught on a side table that jumped at me from out of nowhere, and I flailed for a second. Letting out a whimper, I regained my footing.

"You should sit down, Charlie." Glenda rushed to wrap an arm around my waist and guided me to the sofa. "You're still not recovered fully. Stay here and I'll bring you some tea."

I watched her dart into the kitchen and listened to cups cling around as she rampaged through the cabinets. When I woke up ten hours after the bloodsucker left with the threat

The High Priestess

he would be coming back, I made Tia and Glenda tell me everything that had happened the night we were attacked by the shadow. According to both of them, Nigel the son of a biscuit Thatcher was the knight in shining armor that night.

Apparently, the human police had gotten involved—thankfully after I had destroyed the metal-eating shadow that reeked of death—and pulled over the car that had been no more than a few pieces and a frame in the end. Tia was very animated and used a lot of choice words when she told me that the cops wanted to make it out that it was her fault we were speeding down the streets of Norfolk. They were trying to say she was driving under the influence. They even checked to see if she'd stolen the car and that was why she was being a maniac on the roads. All the accusations were null and void after Nigel turned on his charm and cranked it up to a thousand. He'd convinced them the car's computer had malfunctioned forcing the vehicle to gain speed on its own while the breaks were not working. Before the cops left, they praised Tia for being an amazing driver and making sure no one got hurt. Obviously none of them checked on me while I was half dead in the back seat.

The part that disturbed me the most was my friends telling me that Nigel not only had helped them, but he had taken care of me, too, not even allowing anyone to touch me. Not even Tia and Glenda. Despite Tia's bleeding romantic heart clouding her judgment, I doubted she would lie to me. The bloodsucker had been telling the truth about me thrashing around and only calming when he touched me. Since no trace of the shadow had been left after the last blast of magic I slammed at it, I couldn't blame my restlessness on that. I also remembered too clearly how good and safe it felt while he had his arms around me to keep me steady while all the magic was oozing through my every pore.

My head was hurting from all of it.

"Here." I flinched when a mug of steaming tea was shoved under my nose.

"Where did you say Tia went?" Blowing away the steam, I peered at Glenda over the rim of the mug.

"She didn't say." Shrugging, the seer arranged her limbs on the sofa opposite me, pulling the dress over her knees and tucking it under them. "All she said was 'I'll be back' with that weird accent from the movie *Terminator*."

Typical Tia.

"Was she dressed normal?"

"She wasn't wearing assassin gear if that's what you're asking."

I blew out a sigh and my shoulders relaxed when I heard that. I wouldn't put it past my human friend to take it upon herself to do a sidekick mission, as she liked to call them. My biggest fear was that she'd do something dimwitted like get herself killed and it'd all be my fault. I selfishly dragged her into my world without thinking, and now she would be paying the consequences for my actions.

The whispers perked up at the guilt that was drowning me.

"She is not stupid, you know." My gaze jumped to Glenda, who was watching me contemplatively. "I have a feeling that you think Tia is airheaded and stupid."

"I don't think she's stupid." Wincing at the defensiveness in my tone, I burned my tongue with the hot tea in hopes to cover it up.

"You don't think she's bright either, but I'll tell you what you don't see." Smoothing invisible wrinkles over the skirt of

The High Priestess

her dress, she didn't take her eyes off my face. "She is so scared for you that she doesn't care about the danger she puts herself in if it makes sure she is near enough to help you if you need it. All the things she says that you scoff at … she's doing it to get your mind off things and hoping to make you laugh."

"Making me laugh while our lives depend on silence and staying unnoticed doesn't do any of us any good," I muttered through clenched teeth.

"Actually, when it comes to you, Charlie, it does. It helps a lot."

"What's that supposed to mean?"

"You overthink, and you get anxiety when something or someone depends on you. I don't want to say it, but I will. If the responsibility is left on you, fear leaks through your skin like a perfume, and fear makes people act reckless and make mistakes. She is doing what she can to snap you out of it." Tilting her chin up, she didn't back down, not even even when I glared at her. "She's quite brave if you ask me. I don't think I have the guts to talk smack to you when you get the crazed look in your eyes."

"I don't think the two of you understand the crapcakes my life is serving me right now. It's like it's my birthday." Placing the tea on the low table, I scrubbed both hands over my face with a groan.

"Oh, we understand completely." Getting braver, she leaned eagerly forward when I didn't say anything to silence her. "What you don't get is the fact that you can't do everything alone. You need people to help you, but you keep pushing us away. The excuse that you want us safe doesn't work anymore."

"If I locked you both in here, it'de work perfect." The book poked at my magic as if testing it before it started pulling on me to get to it. I ignored the sensation because I was too agitated with Glenda's argument.

"Unless you can lock us out of sleeping and dreaming, there is nothing you can do to keep us away from danger."

"What did you say?" My heart drumming painfully against my ribs, for the first time I paid attention to Glenda's skin.

Her cheeks were sunken, and it made her cheekbones stick out sharper than usual. Dark smudges under her eyes were covered with a concealer that wasn't doing a great job of hiding them, at least not when I focused on them. While I had been stuck in my own head, my friend had been suffering in silence and I hadn't know anything about it. I hung my head and stared at my lap.

"I'm sorry." I told my fingers, though I was busy twisting them into pretzels in my lap.

"Why are you sorry?" Her giggle snapped my eyes to her face. "Stop taking responsibility for everything. Tia had the nightmares even before Nigel sent you to steal the book. Mine started later, but even with that it's not like you can order us not to dream. I just hope we find something soon so you can send that creature back to where it came from. The nightmares are getting worse."

"Worse how?" The fact that I didn't know Glenda had nightmares too spoke volumes of how self-centered I'd become in my quest to find a way to break the bond with the book.

"Mine are not there yet, but Tia wakes up with bruises and deep cuts all over her arms and legs." Shivering, Glenda licked her lips, a clear sign she wanted to say something but was too afraid to do so.

"Out with it." Drumming my fingers on my thigh, I

The High Priestess

stared at her until her shoulders dropped and she looked defeated.

"You are not recovering as fast as you should." She fidgeted with the seam of her dress. "Knowing everything that you've told me, this shouldn't happen."

"What shouldn't happen? To hurt?"

"It's magic, Charlie."

"I don't follow."

"Regardless of the amount, you only used magic. It's in your blood. You're made of it. It could drain you if you use too much of it or kill you if you are attacked by it. But that book bonded with you because you are special. I doubt it'd bond itself to a person just to kill them. Something feels off, and that has to be the reason you are not back to yourself yet. I just can't figure out what it is, so I wanted to offer a suggestion."

"As long as it doesn't make me feel worse, let's hear it." A thought passed my mind, and I stabbed a finger at her. "And no freaking Nigel either. If it involves that son of a biscuit eater, I don't want to hear a word."

"It doesn't involve Nigel." Glenda laughed in my face, while I grumbled under my breath.

"I did research about the Necronomicon. There is this older lady, a seer who took care of me for couple of years before Master Bowman took me in. She has a large library to help with her hobby, herbalism, but it grew and expanded from that into almost a rare collection of ancient texts. That's what she told me anyway."

I cracked my neck to release the pressure building at the base of my skull, and Glenda grimaced at the sound. Rubbing my hand at the back of my neck, I waited for her to continue. Short of dog poop, I was willing to eat or drink anything if it'd help stop the arthritic pain in my bones. It was either that or renting a senior's scooter to take me around. What a picture I would make if I was perched on a scooter that moved two miles an hour fighting monsters while magic blasted out of me. That picture was more mortifying than the time I thought I'd lose a boob while fighting The Magician and his goons.

"After what went down in the magic guild, everyone heard that clan Jansen is in charge for the time being, until a new head of the mage community is selected. Whispers about the Necronomicon spread too, so she wasn't at all surprised when I reached out asking about it. I didn't tell her anything," Glenda rushed to reassure me. "I blamed it on a vision that has been bothering me lately and told her I couldn't understand it."

"Thank you."

I knew I had issues with trust, and it was probably written all over my face that I'd expected her to blab everything out. They did tell Nigel all of it, after all. Giving her a sheepish smile, I picked up the tea and continued sipping it. At first it had a strong herbal taste, but the more I drank the more pleasant it was. Honestly, it was almost soothing.

"Anyway." I frowned when she looked uncomfortable as if my apology was not warranted. She kept talking, though, so I dropped it. "She is one of those who believe the book exists. After she told me about the bloodline of guardians, she said it takes a very strong character to control that magic, but it can be controlled. Knowing how to butter her up, I told her if only they had her to help she would've brewed them the best potion to help them. That's when she told me about a tea that helps with energy when you are dealing with that large of an amount of magic. She even told me the exact recipe to make it, wistfully saying that it was too bad there was no one strong enough to test it on."

The High Priestess

Rolling my shoulders, I wiggled on the sofa, wondering if the weather had changed outside. It was getting pretty warm in the apartment, and I could feel beads of sweat gathering around my hairline. Already feeling like an asp for treating my friends like they didn't matter, I kept my mouth shut because I didn't want to cut Glenda off. She paused and a worried look passed over her eyes, but I blinked and it was gone.

"Do you want me to bring you water?" Wringing her hands, she half lifted off the sofa, but I stopped her.

"No, the tea is great. What else did she say?" Lifting the said tea, I drained it and plopped the now-empty mug on the low table with a cling.

"That given to the right person, the tea will give them stamina to handle any amount of magic the book may throw at them ... as long as the bloodline is the right one." I blinked as she blanched, her wide eyes staring at me with concern. "If the bloodline is wrong, drinking it will kill the person, supernatural or not."

"You okay?" Attempting to stand up in case she got sick, I listed to the side and almost fell off the sofa.

"I have no doubt in my mind that you are the right bloodline," she said through unmoving lips, but sweat was pouring down my face as if someone was dousing me with a bucket full of water. "You are the strongest person I know, Charlie."

"What are you talking about?" Wiping my forehead off the sleeve on my shirt, I tried fanning my face. "Can we open a window? It's stifling in here. Aren't you hot?"

"You are a guardian of the Necronomicon, and even that creature called you sentinel." Glenda was having a moment of insanity or something because she was blabbering nonsense, and all I could do was sit there and listen to it while I sweated so much I couldn't even think.

"Right, let's go with that." My attempt to stand ended with me kicking the low table and landing hard enough on my knees my teeth rattled. I'd have blue patches like blueberries tomorrow from the unforgiving floor. "First we need some air in here because I'm melting."

"Just breathe, it'll be over in a minute." She didn't sound convincing, but finally my brain registered that something was horribly wrong.

"What will be over?" Blinking through the sweat that was stinging my eyes, I turned to look at her. "What did you do?"

"I had no doubt or I never would've given you the tea." She was paler than a vampire facing a Van Helsing incarnate as she hovered above me.

"Oh my God, you tried to kill me?" I gaped at Glenda like she'd grown a second head.

"What? No!" Shrinking back, her knees bumped the sofa and she dropped on it like a rock.

"Okay ladies, I'm back and I bring good news and a hottie." The front door swung open and Tia waltzed in with the biggest smile on her face. It dropped the second she saw me kneeling in the middle of her living room like a prisoner waiting for her execution. "Charlie?"

"She killed me." I stabbed an accusing finger at a pale Glenda before the heat got too overwhelming and I toppled me to the side. Darkness swallowed me whole.

Chapter Thirteen

"You poisoned me!"

"I did not." Rolling her eyes, Glenda folded both arms across her chest. "You are standing there yelling at me, which means you don't look anything like a dead woman at all."

"Just because I didn't die doesn't mean you didn't pour poison down my throat you sneaky little ..." Hissing at her, I struggled to free myself so I could wring her neck.

"The seer makes a very good point, Ms. Jansen." The dimwit holding me back tightened his arms around me, and that made my bones grind.

"Why are you even here, Margie?" Turning my anger on the bloodsucker, I stomped my heel on top of his foot. "It's time for Selena to change your diaper, so go away."

Nigel chuckled.

"I'm pretty sure laughing at her doesn't help." Tia was leaning on the entrance of the kitchen with a slightly disturbed look on her elven face. "I don't think I've ever seen her this angry."

"I don't think anyone has tried to poison me before, that's why," I snapped at her.

"For the last time, I didn't poison you. I helped you." Not looking sorry at all, Glenda huffed in frustration and stomped to the sofa before plopping on it. "You barely crawled around the apartment for a couple of days, Charlie. Now you are strong enough to wrestle with a vampire. All thanks to the tea I made you drink."

"The poison you mean?" Sneering, I wriggled my arms so I could free them, but the dimwit was like iron manacles around me that shackled me to his chest.

"Tea." Her chin jutted out stubbornly.

I wondered what happened to the mousy creature who'd been afraid of her own shadow. Glenda was like someone with a split personality, one moment a timid mouse and the next a stubborn mule making you want to throttle her. I understood why my uncle kept saying people like us didn't have friends. It wasn't because it was a weakness. It was because they'd drive a saint to commit a murder. Plus, Glenda was a natural redhead. Her temper was poking its head out occasionally was my guess.

"I think now is the right time to tell you my good news," Tia chirped, her lips tilting up in a devious smile. "Actually, I have more than one."

I grumbled under my breath, still upset that I wasn't told what I was drinking by someone I thought I could trust, but I would let her say her peace in the hopes that Nigel would loosen his hold. If Glenda's wariness was any indication, she knew I was waiting for the right time to pounce on her. I grinned like a foe at her, enjoying the widening of her eyes.

"I succeeded to send the people lurking and watching the building on a merry chase across town. If their clothing was anything to go by, I'd say they were just like you, Charlie. All dressed in black and their faces covered." Chortling happily, Tia clapped her hands. "They are chasing their own tail."

"The mages found us?" Forgetting all about the seer, I sagged in Nigel's hold, my body growing cold.

"The human is quite impressive, Ms. Jansen." The bloodsucker informed me, his breath tickling my ear. "You have chosen well."

"Why thank you kindly." Puffing up her chest, Tia beamed at him. "At least someone knows how to appreciate my talents around here. Good deeds being overlooked is the downside of being a sidekick, but I'm okay with that."

The sigh that ripped from me came all the way from my toes. "They could've killed you, Tia."

"What you fail to understand, my friend, is the fact that, just like you, they think nothing of us humans." Pushing off the wall where she was leaning a shoulder, she joined us in the living room by perching on the edge of one of the sofas. "Now I know why not having magic at all is advantageous for me as a sidekick. They wouldn't even see me if I was dancing the lambada butt naked in their face."

I frowned at her. "I see you."

"That's why you're my girl." The sad smile on her face twisted my stomach, and I looked down at my feet. I really was a crappy friend. "But as I was saying, those fuckers thought if I didn't exist for them, I couldn't see them. They weren't even trying to hide from me. So, I took my phone and had a full-on conversation with you while pacing in front of the building."

"When did we have a conversation on the phone?" Everyone had lost their minds in this apartment.

"We didn't," she deadpanned, making the vampire

behind me shake from suppressed laughter. "I pretended to be afraid that my apartment was bugged and I was talking to you from outside because it was safer. I swear it was an Oscar winning performance because they nearly broke their legs to rush and find you in Seattle. I made sure I held the boarding pass in clear sight when I told you what time I'm landing there, too." Her giggling was infectious, and I almost choked on my own laughter.

"You are a genius." Glenda pointed at her, and I silently agreed, especially if the mages sent to track me down fell for the lie.

"That's not all." I didn't like the glint in Tia's eyes when she looked at me. "I conveniently forgot to pick up the thermos I had with me after I specifically reassured you that I had the potion that would lead me to you. I even told you I bought enough of it that if by any chance I lost the trail, I'd have enough to make sure I made it to your safe place."

"What did you have in the thermos?" It was Glenda who asked, and she sported a frown on her face.

"The same tea you gave Charlie. Every time you practiced making it, I didn't pour it down the drain. I saved it." You could hear a pin drop after Tia's proclamation.

"How much was in that thermos?" I didn't think Glenda ever looked that green in the face, not even when she fed me that wretched tea.

"Give or take, two gallons." Tia braced, squaring her shoulders and planting her hands on each side of her hips.

"Oh dear fates, you poisoned half a clan." My knees gave out and I was grateful the bloodsucker held me up.

"That will teach them to come after you." There was not an ounce of regret in Tia.

We stared at each other in silence, her not backing down or allowing me to make her feel bad for what she'd done,

The High Priestess

and me with my head spinning from the ramifications her actions would have on all our lives. I thought life had served me rotten lemons when my uncle told me who my first target as an assassin mage was. This just poked the balloon of delirium I'd cocooned myself in to reveal that it wasn't rotten fruit at all. No, it was cow shit disguised as a cake with a pretty bow that all of us were going to eat by the spoonful.

"I like the human," Nigel proclaimed loud enough I jerked in his hold.

"Of course you like the human," I snapped at him. "You are the only one here without a conscience and with murder tendencies."

"Need I remind you, Ms. Jansen, that you were born an assassin mage? A perfect killing machine," he purred in my ear, speeding up my heartbeat. I was glad I managed to elbow him.

"Why are you even here, Nigel? None of this concerns you." Yanking on his arms, I wanted to bite him in my frustration. "Let me go. I'm not going to attack Glenda. I have other things to worry about now."

"I will beg to differ that it doesn't concern me," he drawled, but he did release me, albeit reluctantly. Great, I was starting to sound like my uncle. "And I was invited."

"Which brings me to my second piece of good news." Tia hurried to cut off whatever I was about to say to the bloodsucker.

"You and I have a very different idea of what good news is." Stiffly, I walked to the lone armchair Tia owned and dropped on it while watching the human expectantly so she could hit me with another shocking revelation.

"I found us a safe place to move to that no one can associate with any of us. Those idiots will never find us or the book there. That's why I went to get the hottie, so he can help us relocate."

"You are aware it's called a safe house because *no one* knows where you are, right?" I looked pointedly at the bloodsucker. "The second you told him, that place is very far from safe."

"It's fine if he knows. Glenda had the vision." Tia dismissed my comment with a wave of her hand.

"For someone that found out magic and supernaturals exist a few weeks ago, you sure believe blindly in everything," I groused.

"For someone born with magic, you have no faith at all," she countered, crossing her arms over her chest with a glare.

"Ladies, ladies, if I may," Nigel started patronizingly.

"You may not." All three of us choired at the same time, which earned us a panty-melting grin. The dimple was just an added weapon of destruction for the female braincells.

"The human has a brilliant plan ..."

"The human has a name," Tia grumbled but was ignored.

"... that will buy us the time for you, Ms. Jansen, to gain control of your powers." We all stared at him blankly—well Glenda and I did. Tia was preening as if she needed to forget that he kept calling her "the human." "And you will not have to worry about Selena coming around either. I will make sure of that."

"Did you find out if my suspicions are correct?" I prodded him.

"I'm working on it." Silver streaked through the gray in his irises, and I snapped my mouth shut because I didn't want him to go full-on vamp here with my friends present. I was angry at Glenda for the tea, but I was still aware the

The High Priestess

seer had been traumatized enough by dimwits. No need to add more to that by running my big mouth. I just had to corner the bloodsucker out of her sight and question him.

"It looks to me like you are still deluding yourself with the idea of training me, Margie."

"It's not an idea but a fact, Ms. Jansen." Ignoring the jab, Nigel puffed up like a bird, only the feathers on his chest were missing. "I was delayed for a moment by making sure Selena was preoccupied and didn't have time to check on my comings and goings. The training will start as soon as you are at this new place the human found."

"I keep wondering what I've done wrong to be punished like this." Closing my eyes, I rubbed my forehead. Poison or not, that tea made me feel normal again, but these three were doing everything they could to give me migraines.

"I'll start packing." Tia jumped up, dragging a dazed Glenda with her. I was too tired to argue with her.

"Everything will be fine, Ms. Jansen." Nigel's somber tone made me glance at his face. My throat tightened from the intense look in his gray eyes. "You will not face Selena until you are ready. And I will do everything I can so you are prepared."

"You believe me that she might be the host?" Taken aback, I gawked at him.

"I'd hate to say that she is that power hungry and I didn't see it." Obviously being wrong about something bothered him more than admitting he had a monster bigger than him in his close circle. "But I cannot in good conscience dismiss your claims. Something is not right with her."

"Thank you." Not knowing what else to say, I pushed the words through my lips.

"No need." At my frown, one side of his mouth cocked

up to brandish the dimple on his cheek. "Isn't this what you wanted?"

"Huh?" What was he talking about?

"Trust, Ms. Jansen." His smirk grew as I stared at him gobsmacked. "It works both ways, as you said, so here I am. For the first time in my long life, I will offer my trust. Don't let me down." He winked.

It really was the end of the world and we were all going to die.

Nigel freaking Thatcher just told me he trusted me.

Me. The assassin he himself hired to kill him.

I could've been having nightmares and eventually I'd wake up, but I had never been that lucky to begin with.

Chapter Fourteen

I squeaked when a hand wrapped around my shirt and yanked me out of the sportscar that I couldn't name—although the symbol in the center of the hood looked familiar—as soon as it stopped in front of a two-story house nestled far from the main road that was surrounded by trees. We drove a couple of hours outside of the city, leaving behind the salty tang in the air along with everything we should've been doing. Instead of looking for Nira before it was too late and a bigger monster came through looking for her, here I was playing house with a human, a seer afraid of her own shadow, and a bloodsucker. My parents must've been turning in their graves.

Gravel crunched and pebbles were joyfully bouncing off the bottom of the car and rolling to a stop just behind us. I got stuck riding with Nigel, while Tia and Glenda followed behind us in a long black sedan courtesy of the smirking vampire peering at me to judge my reaction. The car was so large that my human friend Tia's petite frame in the driver's seat made her look like a middle schooler who had stolen it from her parents and was pretending to be an adult. I could barely see her shoulders through the windshield as she put the vehicle in park and turned off the engine.

Pivoting slowly in a circle, I surveyed the area in the barely visible light from the full moon that was shyly winking at us through the puffy clouds peppering the night sky. After the attack a couple of days ago when the menacing shadow had attempted to devour us and Tia's car, I was seeing foes in every darkened corner. I wiped my sweaty palms on my pants and ignored the intensity radiating from the bloodsucker while he invaded my personal bubble, but the short hairs on my body lifting from his close proximity.

The house looked haunted. From the sharp points and angles of the roof to the boxy look of the exterior walls, it rose from the ground like a sore thumb in the middle of an empty field. Dense trees surrounded it like a necklace circling quite a few yards away, hiding it from anyone passing the road. A wooden porch wrapped around it with thick twisted rafters strategically placed to hold the slanted canopy jutting out from the bottom of the second floor. Windows were sprinkled here and there to point out where the rooms were, and the front double doors were covered in enough dirt and grime to tell me no one had been there in ages. To say it didn't look inviting at all was the understatement of the year. It was the total opposite, actually. It screamed that we needed to get the hell out of there.

The slamming of a car door made me jump and twist to look at my friends.

"Is it safe?" Glenda was still holding the door on her side open while owlishly staring at Nigel.

"It is." His nod came after his narrowed-eye glare inspected the area, but his expression made it seem as if the

The High Priestess

land itself wronged him somehow. "There is no one here but us."

Glenda's messy bun jumped around at the base of her neck while she frantically returned the nod, and then she reached inside the car and pulled the bundle, made of kitchen towels of all things, to her chest. She hugged it tightly like it'd might to escape, her arms curling around her so hard her shoulders hunched a little from the strain. I argued that I should be the one transporting the book, but I had been outvoted when they banded together and told me it wasn't smart to have me and the Necronomicon together because anyone could snatch us both if we were attacked on the way there. We would've still been back at Tia's apartment shouting from the top of our lungs if the sea cucumber next to me hadn't flung me over his shoulder in a fireman carry and dragged me outside.

"I should've zapped him with magic." Still irked by the events, I kept my voice low so Nigel wouldn't hear me, but of course he did. Damn vampire hearing.

The dumbnut chuckled, and the deep rumble of his chest did stupid things to my brain. I clenched my teeth and fisted my hands so I didn't slap him. How he weaseled his way into our trio was still mindboggling to me. It was expected that Tia, as a human, would not be immune to his charms, not when the vampire race was well known for their ability to make people pliant to their whims. They were, after all, the ultimate predators and had many ways to snatch their victims into their webs. It was the seer who left me confused. Glenda didn't trust any male—apart from my uncle for some reason—but as soon as the bloodsucker shimmied his firm behind in front of her eyes she switched loyalties faster than a chameleon changes colors. She said it was the visions, but I had my suspicions because the son of a biscuit eater was scrambling my brain when he was around, too. Nigel Thatcher might be a manipulative, cunning shrimp who was getting on my nerves, but no one could say he wasn't breathtakingly handsome.

And the biggest pain in my tush.

"Who's place is this again?" Uncomfortable standing out in the open longer than was necessary. I edged away from him.

"Mine." Tia skipped as she bounced across the space to reach me. "Well, it's my great aunt's from my mother's side, to be exact, and she's lived in New York for at least a decade. I haven't seen her in longer than that, and we don't have the same last name." Tucking strands of silky hair behind her ear, she craned her neck to look up at the ugly structure. "I forgot all about it until I started looking for places for us to go. She doesn't want to sell it because it reminds her of her husband who passed away long time ago, but she never comes here as far as I know. No one comes here, but she is anal about everything according to my mother, so I'm pretty sure all the bills are paid like clockwork."

"You remembered the house and now magically have a key for this place?" I glanced over my shoulder when Glenda's shoes scraped over the gravel as she joined us.

"No." Snorting ungracefully, she hitched a thumb over her shoulder, plastering a gleeful grin over her face. "That's where he comes in."

"We are breaking in?" I already knew it was a dumb idea, and she just confirmed it for me. "I'm not taking part in this insanity. I'd rather face the clans and Selena, thank you very much."

"You are quite virtuous for an assassin mage, Ms. Jansen," Nigel purred from behind me stalling my need to

The High Priestess

get the heck out of there. "The human is correct. I can't scent anyone being here in a long time. Apart from nature and animals, there is nothing to tell me the house was visited in the last year or two, at least."

Gnawing on my lower lip, I watched the vampire saunter around us and up the few wooden stairs of the elevated porch. They made no sound from his weight, which was promising since no one was taking care of the place, but this was Nigel. He could've been floating for all I knew, and when I walked up there, since I obviously couldn't float, I'd sink right into the rotten wood and he would laugh his ass off. I really wouldn't put it past him.

One thing I had noticed, however, as I held my breath was the silence in my mind. The moment we arrived at this place the whispers quieted to a barely-there hum in my head. It made me feel somehow lighter, as if an oppressive weight had been lifted off my shoulders. I wasn't sure if it was because the book was wrapped up in a bundle, which I doubted, or if it was this place keeping it at bay. I'd heard of areas in the world that were like pockets in space where magic was dulled, but I thought it was yet another myth used to manipulate people. Now, standing in the dark front yard of this old Victorian house, I couldn't help but wonder if there was some truth to it.

The cracking of the unused hinges when Nigel opened the front door were like nails on a chalkboard shattering the silence. Goosebumps popped out all over my skin. I hugged myself and rubbed my arms to erase the chill. Shoving down the need to reach out and take the book from Glenda, I tucked my hands in my armpits as I shuffled my feet a second before a bright light blinded me enough I had to scrunch up my eyes or lose my sight.

"We're in!" Tia squealed right before she tugged on my

forearm hard enough she almost pulled me to the ground. "Come on."

Blinking rapidly to get rid of the bright spots still dancing in front of my eyes, I watched her dart after the vampire, her feet creating a hollow thump on the wooden floor of the porch before she disappeared inside, her platinum hair trailing after her like a flag. Glenda was much slower, still hunched around the book she was hugging to her chest as she gingerly climbed the stairs. Her red hair made her head seem like it was on fire from the bright yellow light blasting my face through the doors. She stopped just outside the front door.

"You coming, Charlie?"

"Yeah ..." Blowing a breath through pursed lips, I shivered before taking the first step closer. "I'm coming."

A rush of warm air washed over me when I stepped through the threshold, the stale air from the house being closed up for so long tickling my nose and making me sneeze. I could hear Tia chatting enthusiastically from deeper in the house, shocked that the bloodsucker was humoring her by laughing at whatever she was telling him. The entrance hallway had a few hooks just right of the door for coats, and a low shelf where they must've kept their shoes at some point. It opened into a long hallway that ended at the back of the house, but there were stairs there leading to the second story. On my right was a decent sized living room with sheets covering whatever furniture was sprinkled around it, and a door leading to a kitchen stood partially open to my left. A couple more doors lined the walls down the hall, all of them closed.

"It needs some TLC, but it's not bad." Glenda pulled me from my observation, my head swiveling curiously despite myself.

The High Priestess

"Until the humans come to arrest us for breaking and entering, you mean?" Rolling my shoulders to get rid of the stiffness, I spun on my heel to look at the few paintings of mountains and pastures on the walls of the living room. "I suppose it's not bad, no."

"Such a pessimist, Charlie." Snorting, the seer walked up to me and bumped her shoulder off mine, still clinging to the book for dear life. "Cheer up, we could use some good things in the middle of the crazy. If nothing else, it'll give us some time to recoup without looking over our shoulder for the clan, or Selena."

"True," I begrudgingly agreed with her, a small smile curling my mouth. "I'm not admitting it to Tia, or I'll never hear the end of it."

"Smart." Glenda giggled, poking her head into the hallway before turning to face me. "Sorry for not telling you about the tea before you drank it."

Noticing the few lined shelves stuffed with random books of all shapes and sizes, I plucked the bundle that Glenda was pressing to her chest and, after pulling off the towels wrapped around it, I shoved it between them. My back stiffened because I expected the temperamental Necronomicon to blast me with some sort of magic for daring to line it on a bookshelf, but it surprised me by being quiet and docile. Between the various novels and encyclopedias, which had escaped the dust that clung to almost everything else in the room, it didn't stand out at all, and I was pleased to be able to hide it in plain sight. Judging by Glenda's sigh of relief, I was sure I'd picked the best place for it.

"Next time you do something idiotic like that, I swear I'll strangle you."

"I won't, I promise, I just wanted to help."

"Everyone wants to help, and I'm the only one always

shaking hands with the reaper for it. Let's not make it a habit." Her face turned all shades of red, but I dropped the subject because there was stomping coming our way.

"It's perfect," Tia gushed as she walked in with Nigel right behind her. "By tomorrow night, we will have it cleaned up. Tonight, we will just sleep wherever we can. There are three bedrooms upstairs, and one main one down the hall here."

"Great, because I'm ready to keel over." I still felt loopy from the poison the seer had given me. "The closest bedroom sounds like a dream."

"They can sleep if they are tired, but not you, Ms. Jansen." The bloodsucker looked smug when my gaze flicked over Tia's head to land on his face. "I will have to go back to the city before morning, so we should take advantage of every minute we have."

"I'm not going to play Cinderella in the middle of the night and scrub the floors, Margie. You can knock yourself out if you want, but I'm off to bed."

"You will not be cleaning." The smile growing on his face made my stomach flip-flop. "We start your training tonight." My pained groan only made the dumbnut grin wider, showing off his fangs.

"It's your fault." I stabbed a finger at Tia's face.

"What did I do? I'm not making you do squat. Yell at him." She turned her back on me.

"You invited the sea biscuit to come with us." Snatching her by the arm when she tried to flee, I dragged her with me outside. "If I have to suffer, you'll be suffering with me. That will show you all the glory of being a sidekick."

Chapter Fifteen

"You need to be faster, girl."

Tia's voice made me grind my teeth as I flipped around in a circle like an idiot while searching for the bloodsucker who was darting around me so I couldn't hit him with magic. I wanted Tia to suffer too by bringing her along, but it had backfired, leaving me with an annoying narrator pointing out everything I lacked while Nigel pummeled me from all sides. I had my suspicions that he just wanted to slap me around but was calling it training so it wasn't that obvious. He couldn't fool me.

"I'm going to send the next blast right at your face if you don't stop talking." Panting, I looked around wildly until I finally zeroed in on the vampire a few feet to my left. "And you!" Pointing the tip of my sword in his direction, I waved it for emphasis. "Stop running like some wuss and stand still for a real fight."

"I am many things, Ms. Jansen, but an idiot I am not." Nigel flashed me a panty-melting grin while circling me. "Your magic is deadlier than ever before. My wish is to train you to use and control it without holding back. This was not a suicidal mission on my part."

"Aren't you a smart cookie, Margie." Honey dripped from my lips as I smiled sweetly at him.

Silver shimmered in Nigel's eyes.

"You are lashing out blindly, focusing too much on catching me off guard instead of actually fighting me." If anyone told me I'd be lectured by Nigel Thatcher on how to kill someone with my magic, I would've laughed in their face a few weeks ago. "You are holding back."

"I'm not holding back." Resisting the urge to stomp my foot like a toddler having a tantrum, I glared at him, twirling the swords in my hands.

"You totally are holding back," Tia mumbled as if pretending she was talking to herself, though she said the words loud enough for me to hear her.

'Tia." Putting as much warning as I could into her name, I grunted when Nigel materialized next to me, his fist connecting with my side.

My poor ribs protested as I scrambled to get away from him while slashing one of my swords in a wide arch that missed him completely. He chuckled, dancing away from my weapon way too graceful than he had any right to be. It wasn't too bright where we chose to do my training. The lights coming from the house were casting the faraway patch of land in a faint glow with enough visibility that I could still rely on my sight to find the bloodsucker. Not that it helped me much. The vampiric speed and strength of Nigel left me gasping for air and standing on shaking legs. Tia, on the other hand, was stretched out on the dirt with her arms propping her up so she could watch me receive the beating of my life.

"I can do this all night, Ms. Jansen." His voice came

The High Priestess

from right behind me, and the breath he didn't even need tickled my ear.

Without thinking, I flipped my right sword so that I held the blade pointing backward, and then I stabbed behind me with the strength of a hammer kissing an unassuming nail. I didn't stab the son of a biscuit eater, but he didn't escape unscathed, either. I felt the tug on my blade when he flashed away, and the sound of tearing fabric filled the air. I spun around wide-eyed expecting to find a trail of blood leading me to wherever he disappeared to.

"Better." Nigel spoke from behind me, and when I spun to face him, he was poking at the rip in the fabric of his shirt with an unenthusiastic finger.. "If you had used magic, you could've incapacitated me long enough to be able to kill me. You are still holding back."

"Okay, fine." Sweat was dripping down my face because my magic throbbed underneath my skin. "If you die, I'll just bury your body by the trees. No one will find it there." Wiping my drenched brow with my elbow, I took a fighting stance, my knees bending slightly and all the weight pressing on the balls of my feet.

"Let us try." Inclining his head regally, all humor deserted the vampire's face. His cheekbones sharpened, and his upper lip raised to reveal a pair of razor-sharp fangs.

My heart did a somersault in my chest before insistently kicking at my ribs like a donkey on steroids. An uncomfortable burn spread over my skin, my magic stubbornly pushing at me to be released. I held back, pivoting slowly when Nigel moved so that I could keep him in sight. Flexing my fingers over the hilts of the swords, I waited for him to make the first move. I didn't have to wait long.

Nigel zoomed past me, dead leaves dancing a foot off the ground in his wake. The blast of wind created from his speed lifted strands of my hair until it twirled it around my face. I stayed as still as possible while keeping my breathing as even as possible, but it was hard because of the fast heartbeat drumming against my lungs. I managed, though. Slow breath in, slower breath out. His body was a blur, just a passing shadow at the corner of my eye, but I only saw it if I was focused on it. But staying calm and in my own Zen bubble allowed me not to just see him but to hear him as well. The whoosh of air when he sliced through it. The crunch of rocks and leaves pressing against the soles of his feet.

As soon as the blur of his shoulders was out of sight, I whirled around and stabbed both swords in front of me to unleash the magic prickling under my skin. Blue electricity crackled and hissed from my hands down the blades until sparks spit over the packed dirt. Bright red flames followed, and my swords blazed like holy weapons in the night. Through the glow I saw Nigel's eyes widen before my magic exploded out, sending him through the air right along with me and Tia. I flew backward and landed hard on my back with an *"Oomph"* when all the air was pushed out of my lungs. Meanwhile my human friend skipped over the ground like a pebble flung over a lake, rolling head over heels in the opposite direction.

Trees cracking had me popping up, scrambling to get on my feet and check on both of them. *What the hell is the matter with you, Charlie?* Screaming internally at myself, I rushed first to Tia because my human friend was much more fragile than a vampire, but apart from a few scrapes and road burns on her arms, she was fine. Heck, she was even grinning like an idiot. With my heart in my throat, I left her sprawled where she was and darted to the far tree line to check on Nigel. The fact that he wasn't lecturing me about holding back or being stupid sent a fresh wave of fear through me. *Please let the annoying son of a cracked nut be alive*, I prayed as I searched around the tall, wide tree that was ripped off the ground, roots as wide as my waist sticking from the bottom of the trunk like open jaws of a hungry shark snapping at the sky.

Dropping on my knees, I started yanking on broken branches and thick foliage in search of his body. "He might just be unconscious," I muttered frantically, making a bloody mess of my fingers that had scraped off the sharp edges of the splintered tree.

"Much better, Ms. Jansen."

I shrieked to the high heavens when the sea cucumber spoke from behind me, and then I fell face-first into the branches, almost poking my eye out on a damn stick. Strong hands wrapped around my waist and tugged me in the air, and then Nigel was depositing me on my feet. His hands hovered on me longer than necessary. Perhaps he thought my knees weren't strong enough to hold me up, and honestly, they probably weren't in that moment. Pressing a hand to the center of my chest, I panted, sucking gulps of air in. Then I glared at him.

"I wish you freaking died you mother fudging titty chomper." Yanking on my hair, which was stuck to my face from all my sweat, I vibrated with anger.

An eyebrow cocked on his handsome face.

"You ought to seriously work on your swearing, Ms. Jansen. It is painful to hear." He dusted off his jeans, which probably cost more than everything I owned. I dismissed all thoughts of him and struggled to get control of my rage.

"I could've killed you." I had wanted my words to sound like an accusation, but of course they came out as a whimper. I hated the fact that my voice cracked, so pressing my lips in a firm line, I stomped away from him.

My ankle twisted, pitching me forward until I flailed in an attempt regain my balance. A hand took hold of my upper arm and righted me, but I yanked it out of his grip and rushed toward Tia. Nigel didn't say anything, instead following behind me like he was expecting me to trip again. It was honestly a good possibility, but his nearness didn't help to slow my racing heart.

"Ms. Jansen." I ignored his call and moved as fast as I dared to get away from him. "Charlie, wait." Hearing my first name coming from his lips made me pause, but I didn't turn around.

"I appreciate your worry." He tugged me so I turned to face him, but I stared stubbornly at his chin so I didn't have to meet his eyes. "I should've told you that you cannot hurt me with your magic, but it just never felt like the right time before we started the practice."

My gaze jerked to lock on his. "Of course it can."

"Theoretically yes, but when I asked you to fetch the Necronomicon, my paranoia that you would run and I would have to search for you revealed a couple of interesting side effects." His intent stare made my mouth dry, but I couldn't swallow. "I took your blood." He reminded me of the worst thing I could've possibly allowed as a mage.

The white rose, with its thorns covered in my blood to match the bottom of the soft petals when I stood frozen in the elevator, came to my mind's eye in great detail. I wasn't sure what it said about me when the clearest picture it brought was his lips gliding over the skin on neck instead of the guilt I should feel for my betrayal of the magical race. I gave a vampire my blood, for Pete's sake, and all I could think about was his soft lips grazing my skin.

The High Priestess

"I remember, no need to gloat." I twisted in hopes of shrugging off his hand, which was curling over my shoulder, but he tightened his hold.

"I only wished to be able to track you." Pausing long enough for me to see the truth in his eyes, he continued. "Mage's magic, including assassin mage magic, is quite painful to me, Ms. Jansen, but it will not kill me. I am too old for it to have a deadly effect on me." My mouth opened, but he beat me to it. "Even before I took your blood."

I grunted because I was completely unconvinced.

"What I discovered, however, the night I came rushing to help you in the ' guild was quite interesting."

"Was it my blood that made you survive the blast The Magician hit you with?" My body shivered, a tremor raking up my spine from the memory of that night. "His magic was not normal, not even deadly like mine. It was tainted ... wrong."

"I believe your blood protected me from it. It is the only explanation I could come up with." Nodding thoughtfully, he searched my face. "I could also feel your powers grow after you created the bond with the Necronomicon when I came to in the hotel."

"What are you saying?" Taken aback, I yanked my shoulder out of his hand. "Not only can you track me like I'm a microchipped pet, but now you can tell what's happening inside me as well? How convenient for you, Margie."

"I can also tell how pure your soul is, unblemished by obsessive ambitions or hunger for power." His hand lifted and he reached for my face, but I stepped away and it dropped to his side.

"Go ahead, start making fun of me. You won't be the first."

"Whatever for?' It was his turn to move back so he could give me an incredulous look. "I'd say it's quite refreshing, Ms. Jansen. It's what helped me make my decision."

"What decision?" Sucking in a deep breath, I finally started feeling all the aches and pains through my limbs. "You know what? Never mind, I don't care, actually. All I care about right now is a bed. Bye Margie, go home." I walked away.

"To help you and to protect you." He stayed where he was and spoke softly to my back.

Tia was shuffling her feet and looking everywhere but at the two of us, even though she was far enough away that I knew she couldn't hear our conversation. Taking a deep breath, I debated if I should turn around and get to the bottom of this insanity the bloodsucker suffered from, but I honestly felt tired all the way to my bone marrow. Judging by the way Nigel kept popping up like we were best friends whenever he felt like it, I knew I'd have plenty of time to talk later. I started walking away again without turning around.

"You should be the last person protecting me, Margie. Go home." A deaf person could hear the weariness in my tone.

"And yet, protect you I will, Ms. Jansen." His voice floated around my head as if he had whispered the words directly in my ear. The bloodsucker never did anything that didn't help him in some way so whatever his reasons were for hanging around, he would be sorely disappointed when he realized I had no intention of letting him manipulate me for his own gain. When I glanced over my shoulder, there was no trace of him anywhere in the area.

Nigel Thatcher was gone like he'd never existed.

Chapter Sixteen

Two weeks.

    For two weeks we lived in our own bubble hidden in the ugly house that was slowly becoming our home. After Tia and Glenda cleaned it up from top to bottom, it actually didn't look that bad at all. Thanks to a certain sea cucumber, as I had started calling him, I couldn't help my friends with the cleaning. I was stuck practicing all night and catching up on sleep during the day. Tia kept pestering me to start calling it home instead of "the house," but I still cringed every time I walked by the pictures of her great aunt pinned to the wall in the second floor hallway because it felt like the human woman was staring me down accusingly for taking over her home. And the large woman looked like she would be scarier to face in real life than Nigel himself.

    The sound of the sawing machine whirled from one of the rooms as I walked past on my way to the front yard, Tia and Glenda chatting happily while they worked on a project I wasn't allowed to see yet. I was sure it'd give me an aneurism when I did see it, so the longer it took, the better it would be for my health. It was nearing sunset, which meant Nigel would be appearing like an unwanted pimple I couldn't get rid of no matter what kind of cremes I used. My heart thumped excitedly at the thought, but I squashed the giddiness down with the determination of a mule. It was just my stupid hormones reacting to the nearness of a predator who used charm and pheromones to butter up his victims, that was all. I considered myself a smart woman, so there was no way I was dumb enough to get attached to the one person who could sell a bag of empty air to Loki the god of lies.

In all the craziness, as much as I didn't want to admit it, I was making very good progress on controlling my magic. My bond with the book, which used to drive me insane by sending crazed whispers through my mind, had strengthened, and now I could communicate with it by using sense of its energy alone. I could tell when it was getting restless or when it needed to dispel a collection of excess magic, when it felt something needed my urgent attention or when it simply wanted to reach out to confirm I was okay. That last part was a little unnerving, but I got used to it too. Tia's trick with the clans was successful as well. We hadn't heard a peep or seen a sign of them yet. I had chosen to ignore the tidbit that she might've killed them with the tea Glenda had made, at least those stupid enough to fall for her trap.

Stepping out, I closed the door behind me with a click, hugging my torso tightly when the cold wind lashed out playfully. It was the end of autumn, and winter was impatiently nipping at its heels as if reminding it to leave. The air smelled like snow, but it was still early for the world to cover itself with the white plush blanket nature knits for it every year. We had a few more weeks to go, I hoped. As

The High Priestess

hotblooded as I was since my magic kept me warmer than a regular human, I wasn't that fond of freezing temperatures. I preferred spring and the cool breeze over frost and icicles. My breath misted the air in front of my face as I looked around to see where Nigel was. He had a tendency to lurk like a creep until he could catch me off guard, and he did that just so he could gloat

An owl hooted in the distance.

After standing on the porch longer than I liked, my body was going numb from the bite in the air, so I pushed off the rafter and trotted down the few stairs. The bloodsucker was late, which was unusual for him since he had arrived like clockwork the past two weeks. That thought made my blood boil, but it also frustrated me to no end. I shouldn't have been paying that much attention. I didn't need him to practice. There were enough trees around, and I was sure the girls wouldn't mind if I scorched a few of them while practicing my precision. I'd probably burn them to a crisp, actually, especially since I still struggled with letting the proper amount of magic funnel through me. Still, I was certain no one would say a word, least of all Tia, who was really enthusiastic about my destructive tendencies.

Reaching the place I usually had my practice, I shook my arms to regain some feeling in them and twisted my shoulders left and right to warm up. The stretchy, comfortable fabric of my yoga pants and long-sleeved shirt was thick enough to ward off the wind, but it wasn't enough to keep me toasty outside. Jumping up and down, I made my blood rush through my veins and my body temperature rise just enough to make me stop shivering. My practice started by sending tendrils of magic at some smaller branches a few feet away. When that wasn't enough, I pulled back to create more distance before attempting it again and again.

My arms burned and my thighs were trembling after jumping, rolling, and pouncing while I fought invisible enemies. In all that, the nagging feeling that I was out of time and things were about to hit a new low for me was like an insistent fly buzzing around my ears. Something was stirring, but I couldn't tell what yet. The calm feeling of my familiar routine was disturbed when the air around me shifted until it was charged with tension so thick I thought if I reached my hand out that I could touch it. Stiffening, I pretended to continue with my form, but my awareness stretched out from me to search for whatever had disrupted the quiet night air.

"You are getting much better at the form your body takes, Ms. Jansen." Nigel spoke a moment after I recognized his power blasting and saturating the air I was pulling into my lungs.

"You're late." My lips pressed into a firm line, and I wanted to slap myself for sounding like I actually cared if he showed up or not.

"I had a little ... delay on my way here." Oblivious to my turmoil, he tucked his hands in the pockets of his pants.

My eyebrows shot up when I realized he was wearing slacks and a button-down shirt, the suit jacket conveniently missing so his muscular body was on display. If he wasn't late by a few hours, his choice of clothing would've told me he wasn't here to help with training. Twirling the swords, I let them disappear by pulling them inside me after they turned into a shimmering mist. I looked at my hands so he didn't catch me gawking like a besotted fool.

"You didn't have to come if you were busy." Waving him off, I swiped an elbow over my forehead to clear the dripping sweat, which always gathered there when I used

The High Priestess

large amounts of magic. "As you can see, I'm fine practicing on my own."

"I had a meeting with your uncle." That got my attention, and I spun around to look at him.

"And?" When he kept staring at me with those smoldering eyes of his, I huffed in annoyance. "Do I need to pull the words out of your mouth by force or are you planning to tell me why? If it wasn't important, I have a feeling you wouldn't have told me where you were. I mean, I'm not your keeper."

"All clans have been mobilized to search for you after the seven who were dispatched to bring you in were reported dead." My heart jumped to the back of my throat and lodged there like a fist while I gaped at Nigel. "It seems the human was successful where many supernaturals have failed because she disposed of seven assassins singlehandedly without giving a clue of who was to blame for their deaths. The mage community is literally chasing their tail on this one."

"If Master Bowman wasn't going to kill me before, now he will not just end my life but make a public spectacle of it to warn anyone else from attempting something similar." There was not enough air in the open space for me to fill my lungs to breathe.

"He was actually quite worried about you." Nigel tilted his face up to watch the gray clouds chasing each other in the starless sky. "If I judged him correctly, I'd say he was even afraid that he would never be able to see you again while he is alive."

"You think I should just waltz in the mage's guild and go give him a hug so he doesn't lose sleep over my wellbeing?" Snorting, I scrubbed both hands over my face. "I'm doomed. This is worse than him knowing about the Necronomicon and my bond with it."

"I said he was worried about you, not about your well-being, Ms. Jansen." My head snapped up at his words, the fast movement sending a sharp pain stabbing through my neck and shoulder. "As for the book ... I'm almost certain he knows. He hinted too much around it for me to think that he isn't well informed on the matter. I'm sure it is the main reason for his concern about your whereabouts. I was given an offer to join the search party and bring you to him."

"Is that why you were late? Because of my uncle and whatever is happening with the clans?" I turned to glance at the house that quietly sat in the middle of the empty field. "Unless you took the job and are planning to drag me back, I'm done being a sitting duck. We need to move from here. They are not safe as long as they are around me."

"I was late because Selena took it upon herself to follow me tonight." Not answering the important question, he spoke evenly and without inflection. If he kept dropping bombs like that, I had no doubt in my mind that I'd end up with whiplash. "It took some maneuvering to lose her and leave her chasing a cold trail."

"I shouldn't be here hidden from everything that's happening in the city. I shouldn't be playing house with my friends." Snarling and balling my fists at my sides, I started pacing. "It's all because of me, because of what I did. My uncle, the clans, Selena ... I shouldn't be chilling here while everything is going to hell there, not when people are dying left and right."

"I would still like to keep you away from it as long as possible." The sound of my teeth grinding permeated the air, and he waved me off, dismissing my furious reaction to his dumbnut comment. "Not for the reasons you think, Ms. Jansen. I assure you I'm well aware just how capable you are to face whatever comes your way. I'd just like to observe them a little longer."

"You want me to hide so you can watch the drama?" Shaking my head, I started walking toward the house. "You need a hobby, Margie. I'm done hiding. It's time to face the music."

"You make me sound like an old aunt, Ms. Jansen." Chuckling, he followed behind me at a smooth pace. "I'd like to observe them longer because at the moment they are panicking. And that makes them, at least in some cases, reckless, like your uncle, or too brave for their own good, like Selena. They are opening themselves up to display their weaknesses, and I'm planning to capitalize on the situation."

"Good for you." Stomping angrily, I climbed the wooden stairs of the porch. "Go play 'I Spy' with my uncle while I make sure my friends are as far away from here as possible, and I will go find Nira before her boyfriend decides to come to our world and turn us all into pulp, okay?"

The tip of my sneaker bumped into the top step of the porch, painfully squishing my toe back into my foot. I swallowed the shout that wanted to rip out of my chest, but a muffled shriek escaped as I bit hard on the inside of my lips. Gravity reached out to embrace me, and I started going down way too fast to be able to stop myself from giving the floorboards a hug. Squeezing my eyes shut, I twisted my body to the side, hoping to take the brunt of the fall on my shoulder and hip instead of my boobs and face. The world spun through my closed lids, and the back of my head, as well as my lower back, pressed heavily on the soft pads of Nigel's hands.

Blinking, I gasped when I saw how close his face was to

mine while he cradled me a quarter of an inch from the grime-covered floor. I could see silver streaks pass through his irises, and there was nothing I could do to hide the jackhammering of my heart from him, especially when it was lifting my shirt with it. His gray, silver-streaked gaze flicked from my eyes to my lips and back, drying whatever moisture I had left in my mouth. Unable to speak, I stared at him wide-eyed, my lips parted for a gasp I couldn't manage.

"On anyone else, this clumsiness would be annoying," he murmured, his lips grazing mine with each word. "For the life of me, I don't understand how it makes you so adorable, Ms. Jansen."

"What?" I spoke so eloquently that cringed and hoped the ground would open to swallow me whole.

"I am going to kiss you now, Charlie." Nigel's eyes burned with so much intensity that dark spots danced at the corners of my eyes. I struggled for breath and panicked that I was going to faint.

I wasn't worried that I'd be unconscious while he was here alone with me. What made me panic was that the sea cucumber would turn it around to feed his ego and claim I fainted because he kissed me. He was arrogant enough to believe it, too, and he would hold it over my head until the day I died. And after hearing everything he'd said, that might not be that far in the future. He was so close now that only a breath separated our lips. Despite my mind screaming at me and calling me all sorts of stupid, my eyelids drifted closed and I licked my lips.

Nigel stiffened above me. "I guess I didn't hide my tracks as well as I thought I did."

Chapter Seventeen

If I had any doubt about whether Selena was a host for Nira or not, it all evaporated in the next few seconds. Unreasonable fear saturated the air around us until I was drenched in cold sweat. My instincts were screaming at me to run, but at the same time they were telling me that no amount of hiding or fighting would help to save my life. A husky, familiar laugh echoed around us, bouncing off the trees and sinking sharp claws of terror into my lungs.

It was hard to breathe.

My fingers spasmed where I gripped Nigel's upper arms when he caught me so I didn't faceplant on the porch, something that he didn't notice because he was too preoccupied by with his own reaction. Silver glittered in his irises and his upper lip was peeled back in a snarl, which placed those sharp, deadly fangs way too close to my face.

I flinched.

It wasn't necessarily a reaction because I feared him. I had stopped being afraid of Nigel Thatcher somewhere between day six and seven of our training when I continuously kept sending him crashing into trees and scotching his clothing. It was a natural-born instinct that was automatically triggered when death was staring you in the eye, and I'd never seen him look as terrifying as he did at that moment. The fact that he was still holding me pinned to his chest and looming over me didn't help either.

A blast of magic barreled into the crown of my head, the book waking up and voicing its displeasure. Instantly my skin felt like it was on fire, stretching and bubbling while magic rushed to fill me up so I could protect it better. That was the only thing that helped me regain control of myself and push away the fear trying to choke me from the inside out Blinking fast, my gaze darted everywhere it could in search of something I could use to snap the bloodsucker out of it without zapping him into a daze, which would certainly happen if I used the power coursing through my veins. I needed him to get off me, not to waste precious time fighting him. The sharp angles of his face and his muscles turned to granite under my fingers, which told me I'd have to fight him if I couldn't get him to see reason.

My friends screamed from inside the house.

It was a horror-filled sound that punched me in the chest and pushed all the air out of my lungs. With no options left, I locked my gaze on Nigel's and didn't give myself time to overthink my actions.

I kissed him.

It wasn't a nice, romantic kiss either. I was too far gone in my panic for that. It was a crash of lips and teeth, my tongue forcefully pushing around his fangs until it scraped them and the coppery taste of my blood filled both our mouths. His shock was a thing of beauty, and if I had time to gloat about it I would, but the only thing I could think was that I'd brought him back.

The High Priestess

The stiff muscles under my hands softened, and Nigel wrapped himself tightly around me, taking control of the sloppy kiss I'd initiated. His lips turned pliant as he molded his mouth over mine, and the sensual way he twirled his tongue around mine short-circuited my brain. My back arched, and I moaned into his mouth, which only elicited a feral groan from deep in his chest. One of his thighs slid between mine to put pressure on my pulsing need for him, and my hips rolled up to chase him when he shifted. His hold on me tightened as if being pressed to each other from head to toe was not close enough for him. The urgency and fear that made me frantic was replaced by insatiable lust, and I clawed at his arms and shoulders, my fingers reaching to tangle in his hair so I could match the ferocity of his need.

The front door crashed open.

"Charlie!" Tia's shrill scream jackknifed my legs and my hipbone nailed Nigel right in his sensitive bits.

Rolling off me with a pained groan, he curled on the porch steps, all silver disappearing from his eyes before he scrunched them closed. A pinched expression covered his face. My mind cleared, the daze his touch and kisses were clouding it with disappearing in a blink of an eye, and then my head jerked back so I could look at my human friend upside down. Her hair was wild around her head, and her eyes were so wide I was worried they'd pop out of her head.

"Now you find the time to fuck?" she snarled at me, and I was left gaping at her while my face burned in embarrassment. What the hell was I thinking? "You had all the time in the world to get in his pants for two weeks. Now your hooha will have to wait because Glenda is losing her shit." Whirling around, she disappeared inside the house, though she left the door open for me.

I scrambled to my feet, kneeing one stair, scraping my elbow, and smacking my chin on the porch in the process. My teeth hurt, and I accidentally bit the side of my tongue, so when the sea biscuit picked me up and set me on my feet, he didn't get the tongue lashing he deserved. Bolting inside the house, I booked it straight for the room where my friends were sewing earlier, finding Tia holding onto Glenda's arms for all she was worth, while the seer was doing everything she could to push her off and scratch at her own skin. She was a bloody mess, for sure.

I dove for Glenda, barreling into the duo hard enough to send Tia crashing into the table where a large sewing machine was perched. Bulks of fabric fell over her until she was buried under them. Taking hold of the seer's wrists, my mind searched for a plan, for what I needed to do next, but all it did was hurt my brain. She had a terrified look on her blanched face, and her dark, forest green irises were hidden by the blown-up black pupil overtaking the color. Fear oozed out of her like a living thing, and I could almost physically touch it. I couldn't think of any other alternative, so I did the only thing I could think of. I slammed a blast of my magic at her, just an energy blast, holding back the electricity and fire because I only wanted to knock her out. She went limp in my hold, and I lowered her before checking on Tia. Both were out for the count, and Tia's forehead smudged with blood from where she must've hit her head on the table. At least they couldn't hurt themselves, although she'd have a killer headache when she came around. *If all of you are still alive.* My mind didn't miss the chance to add that little doubt.

A loud crash outside rattled the walls of the house.

My feet barely touched the ground as I ran to the living room to make sure the Necronomicon was safe. Unable to stop myself in time, I ran right into the back of the armchair, knocking all the air out of my lungs with a whoosh. My chest hurt as I choked and coughed, and then I sucked in a breath that froze in my throat when I noticed half of the wall where the window had been facing the front of the house was missing. Nigel was sprawled out over the rubble, a thick part of a broken beam piercing his stomach. He stirred, but dark shadows moved in the gaping wall and my eyes snapped in their direction.

There was no mistaking the emblem on the black clothing of the three assassin mages that stepped into the light where I could see them. The two dragons wrapping around each other announced loud and clear that clan Jansen was done chasing their tail. They had found me, and judging by the venomous glint in their eyes, they were not here to take me back. No, they were here to kill me. For some stupid reason, my shoulders relaxed when I saw them. With the irrational fear blasting us earlier, I thought Selena had found us. I wasn't entirely sure I could win against her if she was indeed a host for Nira. Assassins from my clan, though, I could fight any day. A creature from nightmares from another world? Not so much. Even I was not that delusional, regardless of my bond with the book and the blind faith my friends gave me.

"Master Bowman sends his regards." One of the mages spoke as he stepped forward, wicked daggers materializing in his hands.

Nigel groaned.

As much as I wanted to check on the sea cucumber, I couldn't take my eyes off the three dimwits who had come to kill me. If he was making noises, that meant he was still alive. I shouldn't have cared as much as I did, but whatever. The frantic beating of my heart had slowed, at least.

My swords slid out, the weight of their hilts settling comfortably in my hands. From the corner of my eye, I glanced at the bookshelf to reassure myself that the book was still where I had left it. Focusing fully on the one who spoke, I offered him a crooked smile.

"Aww, Astor. I knew you'd miss me you son of a biscuit eater." Rounding the armchair, I stepped over broken pieces of wall, glass shards, and flipped-over furniture until I stood between the bloodsucker and the mages. "Couldn't wait to come and say hi, huh?" I almost tripped over a particularly wide piece of plaster, and the two behind him snickered at me.

"Your end has come, Charlie," Astor snarled, gliding closer as the other two mages fanned around him as if to surround me.

"Jonas let you wander around alone?" Adding as much mockery as I could to my tone, I kept an eye on all of them while pulling magic inside me with gusto, the book adding its fury to mine. My skin was stretched so thin that my body was vibrating from it. "Look at you all grown up, you mother fudging titty chomper. I knew you had it in you."

"You can't win, Charlie," Astor gloated, pulling his hood and covering down to reveal his ugly mug. "Jonas couldn't be here, but I'll have the honor. My face will be the last you see before you die."

"Pull that thing up, will you? I'd rather look at a donkey's ass than your face." Shivering for emphasis, I grinned at him when his face twisted into a furious grimace.

A ball of fire as large as my head came sailing from the side, and I ducked just in time to miss it, though a few strands of my loose hair sizzled until the stench of burning hair filled my nostrils. The fireball crashed into the still standing wall and flames licked the wallpaper. I sent a blast

The High Priestess

of magic at it, the boom it created extinguishing them instantly. My heart rattled in my chest. The dumbnuts would burn the house, and the book right along with it.

"Fireballs? Seriously?" My gaze darted around the room to find a way to drag them away from here. "You must have a better imagination than that."

"The time for talking is over, kibitzer." One of the other two mages hissed before a tendril of bright orange magic shot from his hand and wrapped around my waist.

It burned like hell, and it definitely took my breath away. I couldn't stop the scream that ripped from my chest. The world spun around me when he tugged hard, my body tilting to the side. I slashed wide with my sword to slice through his magic before stumbling to regain my footing.

They laughed, all three of them.

Behind me, slabs of plaster shifted and puffs of dust filled the air like fog. It distracted the mages enough that when I sent an entire sheet of blue electricity at them, only Astor managed to roll away. The other two dropped on the ground, their bodies spasming on the dirt-covered yard. Unwilling to lose my advantage, I sent wave after wave of blue magic at them, keeping Astor rolling around to avoid it like a happy pig playing in the mud. The two other mages thrashed on the ground, their screams feeding the glee I felt from the Necronomicon before abruptly quieting. Silence fell on all of us.

Astor popped up on his feet, his black clothing looking almost white from the plaster and brick covering the ground he was rolling on. His face paled when he glanced around at his dead friends before snapping his gaze to mine. I didn't have to see my face to know my smile was terrifying because his face turned a ghostly white right before he bolted out of the front yard must too fast. I didn't think anyone but a vampire had that kind of speed. Holding my breath, I waited to see if there were more of them, but nothing else moved. The only sound that disturbed the night then was the occasional cracking from the house. I didn't think anything of being unable to hear the owl hooting from the forest because the bird never missed an opportunity to tell us he or she was watching us day and night, but then Nigel spoke from behind, scaring the daylights out of me.

"Ms. Jansen, get inside the house." There was a pitch to his tone I'd never heard before, so my head snapped around so I could look at him.

He wasn't looking at me, so I frowned at him. "I thought you kicked the bucket."

"Get inside the house, Charlie." His face twisted in fury, and paired with his hunched shoulders, he looked every bit the predator ready to pounce.

"Are you okay, sea biscuit?" For the life of me, I didn't know what was wrong with him. Did he hit his head when he skewered himself on the wooden beam?

"Well enough to deal with that," he spat, pointing at something behind me. When I spotted what he was referring to, all the blood in my body dropped to my feet.

Chapter Eighteen

Clap, clap, clap.

"How impressive, sentinel." Selena's husky voice came from everywhere, and there was a slight lilt to her words that sent tremors through my spine.

The slow clapping of her hands was accompanied by a girlish giggle that sounded all sorts of wrong given the situation. The bloodsucker had tunnel vision, his body poised and ready to attack. All his attention was focused on the woman approaching us with a seductive sway to her hips. Her usual no-nonsense bun was missing, her white hair twisting and twirling around her face like the snakes on Medusa's head. A mark shaped like the crescent moon was glowing bright gold on her forehead, and her floor-length blood red dress was brushing the tops of her bare feet with each step. Her features were blurring and flickering like the picture on a TV with bad reception, and the elder wood wand was twirled between the fingers of her right hand.

"Indeed impressive, Charlie Jansen." The witch leered at me, a wicked smile lifting her red painted lips. "Sneaky,

sneaky," she sing-songed. "Becoming a sentinel, *and* leashing the stud like a dog, I see."

"Hello, Nira." Backing away until I stood shoulder-to-shoulder with Nigel, I called her by her real name. There was no more doubt that Selena was the host, but that wand in her hand was sending all sorts of alarms blaring in my head.

"Splendid!" She bounced on the balls of her feet excitedly, her grin showing so many teeth it was unnatural. "You've heard of me. This makes things much easier."

"Easier for whom, and for what?" Eyeing her warily, my gaze kept dropping to the elder wood. I wondered if somehow I could jump her and knock the wand out of her hand. Things would definitely be easier then.

"If I knew you had been expecting me, I wouldn't have wasted time with those poor excuses for magic users you call family." Wrinkling her nose like she smelled something foul, she shook her head and brightened instantly. "We can come to an agreement sentinel, you and I."

Nigel snarled, so I elbowed him to shut him up. I needed time to think or all of us were going to die. The vampire was arrogant enough to think fighting Selena, now Nira, would be as easy as fighting any other supernatural. But I stood in their world and felt the power they were packing, and that was when Ulthar had been trying to be nice. This creature would kill us before we had time to blink if we didn't outsmart her, so I had to keep her talking until I figured out what to do.

"I will rip you limb from limb, Selena," Nigel snarled, which earned himself a pitying smile from her.

"Selena is not home right now, dear," she told him with so much sincerity it dripped like honey from her painted lips.

"What kind of an agreement?" Bringing her attention back to me, where it needed to be, I was proud I didn't sound like a frightened little girl as I rolled my shoulders and pretended to be relaxed.

"You see, I rather like being in your world." She glided closer, and I had to elbow the snarling sea cucumber again. At least he wasn't attacking, so we had that going for us. "Humans are so very entertaining in their fear, and they feed my needs beautifully. If I promise to keep my play time spaced out to not give you too much trouble, you will promise to look the other way and pretend I am not here." She looked so innocent it set my teeth on edge. "That way we both win."

"I'm not sure your mate will agree with you." Cold sweat was dripping down my spine and drenching my shirt, and the closer she came the worse it got. "You don't belong here, Nira."

Snorting, she waved a hand at my comment in dismissal. "Nodens is such a crybaby. He has Lythalia and Lilith to entertain him. I was bored, you see. I wasn't meant to be tied down, but to be free. I'm sure you understand that."

Banging came from inside the house, and that told me that my friends were coming around. Panic choked me when Selena/Nira perked at that, her eyes flicking over my shoulder with a hungry look on her face. I still had no idea what I was going to do, but my time was up. If I kept blabbing nonsense, Tia and Glenda would come out. I wasn't willing to risk their lives just so I could think of a way to send Nira back where she belonged. Or die trying, as the case may be.

"I'm afraid I can't let you stay, Nira." Taking a deep breath, I yanked for the magic around me and the bond I had with the book with all I was worth. "You have to go back."

My swords burst with bright red flames, blue electricity flickering through them when I raised my hands in preparation of the coming fight. Stepping in front of Nigel, I nudged him so he moved back, but the bloodsucker only slid closer until his chest connected with my back. My whole body was burning from the inside out, and I didn't know how he could handle touching me, but if he wanted to be a roasted turkey that was all on him. Selena was glaring at me with so much hatred that I could hardly even swallow because my mouth was so dry.

"Very well, sentinel." The damn elder wood wand lifted in the air, and my blood curdled. "I will feast on your flesh and pick my teeth with the bones of those you hold dear."

The bond with the Necronomicon blazed bright inside me until it felt like my ribs were cracking.

"After I kill you, I will do as I please." Grinning, she laughed, and her feet lifted off the ground.

I gaped at the creature floating a few feet in the air like gravity meant nothing, her hair lashing out wildly around her head. Her eyes glowed like molten lava, and sharp black talons replaced the nails tipping each finger. Even worse were her choppers, which lengthened and widened until her mouth turned into the jaw of a hungry shark with razor sharp teeth. Shadowy wings with the span of a bus flipped behind her, dripping black goo that sizzled and spat every time it touched the ground.

"Let us play, sentinel." The tone of her voice was scarier than Ulthar's when she spoke. My heartbeat tripled.

"Oh my God." Tia's faint whisper behind me was followed by two loud thumps, but I couldn't afford to inves-

The High Priestess

tigate even though it made me stiffen when the bloodsucker shifted at my back.

"The human and the seer fainted." Nigel's words were slurred around his fangs, and I barked out an unhinged laugh.

"It was nice knowing you, sea cucumber." I snickered, fear making me act like a mental patient.

I didn't wait to hear what he said. Stabbing both swords in front of me and pointing their tips at Selena, I released a torrent of magic like a tsunami wave. It exploded outward, bright red and blue bursting like the sun and slamming into the floating creature with the speed and strength of a falling meteor pulled by the atmosphere. It flung her like a ball hit with a baseball bat, her red dress flaring when she spun head over feet in the air and disappeared into the trees surrounding the property. The loud sound of my blast made my ears ring as I stood blinking at the empty air meeting my eyes.

"That was it?" The question was whispered through my numb lips a little too soon.

A shrill scream pierced the night, and it was filled with rage. My heart stopped when a dark shadow lifted above the tree line, the red eyes glowing in the darkness making me think Satan himself was coming to eat me alive. They were fully focused on me, the intensity like a noose squeezing me by the neck. It stood still for one second before shooting straight at me like a bullet. Twisting around, I shoved the bloodsucker until he sprawled on the ground, and then I dashed out of the house running like my own tush was on fire.

Newsflash, it was on fire big time.

I tripped on a rock and my stomach met the dirt as I skidded over the pebbles for a few feet, my teeth rattling in my mouth. It saved me from colliding with the creature that zoomed over my head like a blast of wind. The air charged with magic, and I recognized the power of the elder wood wand when it lifted the hairs on my arms. It crackled around my ears, and I rolled away through the dirt just in time to avoid the blast. It left a hole in the ground like a freshly-dug grave in the same spot where I should've been.

Lifting on my hands and knees, I crawled away for a few seconds before climbing to my feet and running for the trees. I needed to get her away from the house, and as long as I was alive, I knew she would follow me. Arms pumping, I clung to my swords as I dashed in a zigzag with bolts of magic hitting the ground a second after I moved away from the spot. Dry soil and dirt flew in the air, hitting me in my legs and back as I ducked and swerved across the long stretch of land. Blindly, I flung bolts of electricity and balls of fire over my head, but since her attacks didn't pause, I must've missed my target.

Nira laughed.

Her gleeful chortling made my teeth grind as I threw myself at the trees and disappeared between them. My legs were trembling and burning from the strain as I plastered myself to a trunk, the bark chafing my cheek as I pressed against it. I gasped for air more out of fear than from the running, and I was hugging the stupid tree when the leaves rustled above me. Not missing a beat, both of my hands lifted and thick ropes of magic lashed out, pulverizing the branches and showering me with burning leaves. Nira's pained and outraged scream was a balm warming my frozen insides. I sent another wave of magic up, stepping away from the trunk to give myself a better view of the top of the leafy tree. A thump to my right had me spinning to face that direction.

The High Priestess

"I should've known you'd be a pest," Selena/Nira spat at me, half of her face and the her shoulder melted, but the skin was knitting together as I watched.

I slammed more magic at her, hitting her square in the chest. It launched her back until she slammed into the tree closest to her. She fell in a heap but pushed herself up before I had time to see her on the ground. She dusted off her ripped dress without a care in the world. With determined strides she headed for me and had her hand wrapped around my neck before I realized what was happening. Lifting me off the ground, she grinned at me while my feet were kicking the air uselessly, and my head felt like it will explode from not getting any blood flow in it. My swords dissipated, and I clawed at her wrist in futile attempts to be able to breathe. All my struggles stopped when the tip of the elder wood wand touched my face.

Something barreled into Selena, flinging her to the side. She dropped me and I hit the ground hard on my knees, instantly choking and gasping for air with both hands holding my poor throat. When I blinked away the tears that were rolling down my cheeks, I saw Nigel straddling her, both his arms bulging while he held Selena by the neck. She lifted the wand that she was still gripping in her hand, and I dove for it with a desperation I'd never felt before. All three of us were rolling around on the forest floor. I was trying to take the wand off her, though I almost released her when my fingers slipped on the slime oozing out of her, while Nigel was doing his best to strangle her. Desperate for something to go our way, I did the only think I can think of when I heard the bloodsucker grunt in pain .

I bit her.

My teeth sank into her slimy skin, and it made me gag. Still, I clamped my jaw like a bulldog unwilling to give up his bone. Selena screamed so loud it busted my eardrums open, and in my panic that she'd get herself free, both my hands released her and my swords burst out in my palms. Still biting as hard as I could, my mouth filled with bitter liquid as I started stabbing blindly at her side, powering each hit with magic that I was dragging from the center of my being. Selena was still going strong, but now her talons were shredding my shoulders and chest in her attempt to get me off her. The craziest thing was seeing that she still had a smile on her face as if all this was truly just a game for her. I had no idea how she did it because dark spots danced in front of my eyes as I was slowly bleeding out. Pulling my head up I spat the vile liquid while stabbing the hand holding the wand with one sword and staking it to the ground. Nigel was pummeling at her too, but he was having just about as much luck as I was,

We are all going to die. The thought was loud and on repeat in my head.

Selena froze, and that was the only reason I was able to hear the crunching of footsteps moving fast in our direction. My heart stopped when I heard Tia call out for Glenda to get back to the house and away from the forest. I was about to stop stabbing at the creature when I peered over my shoulder to watch for Glenda, and when she arrived, the redhead skidded to a stop a couple of feet away holding the Necronomicon open in front of her like a sacrifice.

Selena shrieked.

Shadows bellowed out from the open pages of the book, its pull on me strengthening my resolve. I turned to Selena with renewed determination, my body lighting up with the power of the book. The whispers slammed into my head until every other sound was silenced, and then I heard myself speaking in an unrecognizable voice.

The High Priestess

"I banish you from this world, Nira." My words boomed around us with so much power it sucked the air from my lungs.

Both my hands lifted over my head, the billowing smoke from the book wrapping around my swords. Electricity and fire flickered through the twisting shadows as I brought the swords down and stabbed Nira in the chest. The magic exploded, flinging all of us back but leaving Selena screaming with her back bowed off the ground. To be honest, I was shocked she didn't break it. Glenda was crumbled next to the tree, the open book sitting unassuming on the forest floor. Silence surrounded us next, and I knew we all held our breath. At least I was.

A shadowy cloud came from the Necronomicon, and it slithered over the ground until it reached Selena's prone body. It covered her completely while I watched wide-eyed, and when it pulled back, I knew what I was about to see. Or not see, as was the case. The body was gone, and the elder wood wand had joined a pile of broken branches on the ground. I could feel Nigel's eyes on me, but I did everything I could to stop me from looking at him. The shadow crawled back inside the book and a new card was thrown in front of me where I knelt. It fell right in front of my hand holding my weight up.

Sitting back on my haunches, I picked it up, pausing before I flipped it over to see what it was. The High Priestess stared back at me, a demure smile tilting the corners of her lips. Glenda crawled on her hands and knees to see it over my shoulder, sighing heavily before she leaned her forehead on me.

"It's over," she mumbled, patting my back before she stood, grabbed the book, and hugged it to her chest.

"How did you know to bring the book here?" I was still

staring at the card when I asked her. The tips of Nigel's shoes popped into my field of vision.

"I don't know," Glenda muttered softly. "It felt like it was asking me to bring it to you, so I did."

"Is this what happened to The Magician, too?" The bloodsucker took the card from my numb fingers and I looked up at him as he turned it over in his hand.

"Yeah." Jumping to my feet, I turned away from him because I didn't want to answer any more questions.

Glenda was still standing close and hugging the book, so I reached for it, tugging it out of her hold. It slipped from both our hands, tumbling down with rustling pages. My heart skipped a beat a second before it fell between us, its pages facing the sky. Icicles spread through my veins when I saw the picture staring at us. A man carrying a bundle tied to a stick over his shoulder looked too uncaring for what it actually meant for me. Something else must've slipped up through the gate. I felt Nigel come to stand next to my shoulder, and he looked down at the picture, too.

"Which one is this?" the words barely passed my unmoving lips.

"The Fool."

Glenda's whisper made me shiver when I remembered Selena calling my uncle the exact same thing.

More by Maya Daniels

vinci-books.com/restingwitch

Forbidden fruit is sweet… until you take a bite.

I was the dud of my coven—until a failed spell blew up the library and unlocked my magic. In my panic, I tried a simple spell, but instead, I destroyed ancient texts, wrecked half the building, and somehow ended up half-naked in the high priest's office. Now, I'm totally screwed.

Turn the page for a free preview…

Resting Witch Face: Chapter One

Lesson 1: *don't drink and drive.*

No, scratch that. That was for humans. The real lesson was: don't drink and pretend you're something you are not. Like, acting like a badass witch when you have zero magic. Take it from me because it'll destroy your life. Although that was neither here nor there, when it came to me, since I was screwed the day I popped out of my mother's vagina. She died during childbirth, most probably out of disappointment. I kid you not.

I was a dud born in the most powerful bloodline of witches in the world.

How was that for a sap story?

"Hey, buddy," I called out like we're the best of friends. "Get back down here before you hurt yourself and I get blamed for it. What do you say?" The Kishi demon cocked his head and eyed me like I'd lost my mind. Poor schmuck had no idea that ship had sailed years ago.

My foot wobbled in my designer ankle boots when I

The High Priestess

took a step forward, and I did an awkward shimmy-wiggle-swan-dive before I regained my balance. It was what happened when you drank one too many Manhattans and answered a call from your coven to deal with a demon selling illegal merchandise.

"Damn you! If I scratch my boots I'm going to skin you alive just to make myself a new pair. I should've just stayed in the damn bar." The racket of a paint can crashing to the floor and rattling around applauded my muttering. It also stabbed my brain, which was pounding like a shifter in heat when a willing body accidentally stumbled in front of his dick. Don't ask me how I know this, because as brutally honest as I am, I'm not going to tell you.

iPhone held in front of me the same way those pompous asses from the Magi Police waved their badges around, I pointed the flashlight right into the creep's eyes. It screeched like a banshee and scattered further into the darkness while I hissed curses at it. Luckily for the demon, none of them would be taking root, because ... no magic, duh.

What took my coven mates so long to get to the warehouse? If this was a party they'd be lining up at the door since yesterday. As I looked around the dirty warehouse and the misty odor of congealed blood and decaying bodies made my stomach roll, I couldn't say I blamed them.

The fact that Kishi demons had an attractive human face on the front and a hyena's face on the back of their skull was the least of my problems. Kishi demons used their human face as well as their smooth, luring voice and other tricks to attract unassuming idiots— which I definitely was not, shut it I'm not!—and then they proceeded to eat them with their deformed jaws. That would've been fine and dandy if they kept it under wraps, but this one also made an entire collection of body parts to sell on the magical black market. Quite a smart trick when the market was scarce, but not such a great idea for this guy, because he was dumb enough to get caught. That was *if* I managed to hold him back until the others got to the warehouse. With all the alcohol in my blood system, I got this like a hot potato in a bare hand.

Witches more than other supernaturals paid good money for body parts like the ones stacked all the way to the ceiling in the large building, although nobody liked to talk about it. It was that pink elephant in the room we all ignored. No delusions clouded my mind that my coven would "confiscate" the evidence in the warehouse without blinking an eye. I was basically standing in the middle of a gold mine.

The pentagram tattoo on the side of my forefinger tingled, an annoying reminder when my body thought I should be using magic, as adrenaline raced through my veins. My meat suit never got the memo we were shooting blanks. We were as impotent as Mike, my coven's administrator, according to Sissily.

"Go away witch, or die," the demon cooed, his alluring voice gliding over my skin like a caress and leaving goosebumps in its wake.

"Aww, you actually think I'm a witch." My eyelashes fluttered in his general direction as I stumbled deeper into the warehouse. "How adorable," I deadpanned, a serious expression on my face that froze him in his tracks.

Silence followed.

"Ah, you are the useless one." His face poked through the shadows before he fully emerged to sneer at me from over ten feet up, crouched like a gargoyle on the rafters. "I've heard of you. Pathetic." He dismissed me, as his full lip curled over a row of flat, white teeth.

The High Priestess

I hated sneering. It reminded me too much of the looks on my coven mates every time they stared in my direction.

Shaking my head to regain my focus, I swallowed hard when the alcohol tried to come up. All I had to do was keep the hellspawn from escaping until reinforcements arrived, but he was pushing his luck. Even a dud could do that if said dud was not a little drunk and teetering on six-inch heels. I eyed my precious boots for a split second, considering using them as a weapon and chucking them at his head, but I changed my mind. Like hell I would mess up a good pair of designer boots for a stupid demon.

The choice was taken from me when he decided to try a trick called monkey in a circus and sailed through the air, aiming his body straight at me. My phone jerked to follow the arch of the jump, and I had one second of an "oh shit" moment before our bodies collided. Never mind me, my iPhone flew from my fingers, crashed on the concrete floor with a resounding crack, and I heard my silk shirt rip at the shoulder when we tumbled on the dirty concrete floor. I just bought that phone.

I saw red.

Fingers hooked like claws, I went straight for his eyes when he tried to straddle me. Somewhere in the back of my mind I was aware that if he bit me the poison from his kind would kill me in less than an hour, but I had liquid courage, louder than the alarm bells cheering me on. The demon didn't expect me to claw at his eyes, so when my nails made squelching mush out of his eyeballs, his human face roared at me. If I was in the right mind, I would be shaking in my skin. As things were, he resembled a chihuahua nipping at my ankles to my muddled brain. Wretchedly vile breath melted my makeup and I gagged, barely holding back the bile so I didn't puke all over both of us.

"It's called a toothbrush, asshole." I hacked hard enough to cough out a lung while jamming my forearm in his throat to hold back his snapping jaws. The Kishi demon was trying to munch on my face, for fuck's sake. "You should use it, damn you."

Desperate times called for desperate measures, and, as much as it pained me, I had to sacrifice my boots. My leg swung up like a slingshot, caught him on the side of the head, and he went down hard. His head bounced off the concrete, and his skull cracked with enough strength to be heard over the heartbeat in my ears. The air whooshing out of him satisfied my need to hurt him like he hurt my poor blouse. It was also new and cost me an arm and a leg. Using the time I had, I scrambled on my knees, yanked my poor boot off, and nailed him in the neck with the heel. The demon gasped, probably still dazed from the kick, but apart from a few spastic jerks, he didn't attempt to flee. Or move again at all, but that would be semantics.

They might think that was how I found him.

Right.

With a sigh, I dropped on my haunches not a moment too soon before the solid thump of feet came from the entrance behind me. Light jiggled up and down over the stacked shelving from the flashlight the person held, and I looked down my shoulder at the flipping piece of silk that used to be a soft olive color. Dirt, sweat, and dried blood from the scrapes on my upper arm turned the silk some disgusting color of brown. I frowned at the flapping fabric.

"Hands up where I can see them," the owner of the flashlight barked from behind me.

Great. Instead of my coven mates, I had to deal with a human cop. Just my luck for the night, it seemed.

"Do I look dangerous to you?" My head twisted so I

could squint at him over my shoulder, and a bright light stabbed me in the brain like a pickaxe. "Are you trying to blind me on purpose, or is this how you pick up chicks all the time? If they have a flashlight burning their retinas they can't see your ugly face, huh?" Oh yeah, I recognized the voice better than I should've.

"Hazel? What in God's name are you doing here?"

"Getting a tan. You?" I chirped brightly and regretted it when acid filled my mouth. I would never drink again.

"Don't be a smartass. I'm seriously asking what—" His words stopped when he noticed my ripped shirt and one bare foot, and he shuffled closer. I was pretty sure having my skirt bunched up around my hips and flashing the creases of my ass didn't help, either. Goddess, I looked a mess.

"Are you hurt?" His hulking frame kept moving closer, sending my heart to gallop in my chest.

"No, wait." My sudden shout stopped him in his tracks. "Stay there, Davon, you don't want to get bitten." Think Hazel, think.

"Bitten? What the hell, Hazel. Get away from there right now. What's in there?" When a gun cocked, I knew the jig was up. If he saw the demon, there was no doubt in my mind I'd be in more trouble than I already was.

"It's a dog, okay. Stay back because if you spook it, it'll bite me. Then I'll be pissed. Do you want that?" Where the hell was my coven?

"What kind of a dog?" Tone dripping with suspicion, his feet scraped the floor as he cautiously moved closer again. If he saw the Kishi starfishing it, not even my grandmother could cover the mess up.

"You are the one with a flashlight, Davon, so why don't you tell me. I'm not playing games when I tell you to stay back. Look at my face." I added an additional scowl for good measure, shuffling on my knees to hide the Kishi sprawled a couple of feet away, deep enough in the shadows not to be visible for the moment.

"What about it?" I could've laughed at the weariness in that loaded question, but he did stop coming closer.

"Does it say approachable to you right now?"

"It never does," he muttered, and I grinned at him like a fiend. "This is crazy. You don't get to boss me around after you dumped me."

"I already parted with my right boot, and I love these boots. You wanna try the left one? I can nail you in the forehead or in the jingleberries. Your choice," I threatened while internally freaking out. Being a bitch to Davon wouldn't work much longer. It never did. He would do the opposite of what I told him just to spite me. I could feel it.

"Hello," a female voice called from the entrance of the warehouse, and I deflated like a balloon recognizing my best friend Sissily. About freaking time. The demon was dazed, but he wouldn't stay down much longer. And if he woke up with Davon here, I had a nagging feeling my body parts would join those scattered around the warehouse in jars. Courtesy of my grandmother, of course. The demon didn't have shit on her when that witch got pissed.

"Stop right there. Police." Davon pointed his gun and flashlight at Sissily's face. Protecting her poor eyesight with a forearm flung in front of her, she blinked at him as if ready to say something.

"Is this your dog?" I rushed to say before she screwed me over. You never knew what would come out of her mouth. "It might be injured, it almost bit me."

"Hazel ..." Davon started in a warning tone.

"Yeah, oh thank goodness you found him," Sissily

The High Priestess

gushed, overdoing it a little, if you asked me. Whatever Davon wanted to say was silenced, thank the goddess.

"If this is your dog, Ma'am, I must report it, I'm afraid. It attacked a civilian, and it's considered dangerous." Davon, the good cop he always was, started reading Sissily her rights while she rolled her eyes.

I sighed, pinching the bridge of my nose.

"Oh, shut up human." Her hand flicked when she had enough of his word vomit, and she zapped him hard enough the poor guy convulsed a long moment before he passed out, the gun and flashlight clattering on the concrete.

Then she turned her blue peepers my way and gave me a once-over. Although her blonde hair was smooth and all in one place, and her pencil suit was sharp enough to cut a finger off, Sissily had no right to grimace at me. Someone should tell her "I bit a rotten lemon" was never a good look on a chick. Just saying.

"If you say a word Im'ma boob punch you." Pushing off the ground, I swayed, and for the second time I failed to glue the ripped silk sleeve together. "Are you alone?" It was improbable, but a girl could hope.

"The others are not far behind me. I had a feeling you'd jump right into this, so I made sure I came before anyone else. What do we have?" She sashayed closer, giving Davon a disgusted look.

"Kishi demon." I glared at the asshole who finally stirred with a groan.

"How do you find yourself in these situations, Hazel?" Ignoring her, I was still messing with the sleeve, so with a sigh, she took her jacket off and handed it to me.

"Thanks." Limping a couple of steps forward, I plucked it from her fingers. "And I wasn't kidding about the boob punch. I'll even twist your nipple until you scream if you don't keep your voice down."

"You do know we're not five anymore, right?"

"What's your point?"

I could tell she had so much to say just by the tightening of the tendons on her neck. Her throat worked, her mouth opening and closing until she gave up and shook her head.

Yeah, exactly my sentiments.

"Where's your other boot?" She followed the elaborate swirl of my finger until it pointed at the demon. My beautiful, precious boot was sticking out of his throat, covered in black blood and gore. Then she arched an eyebrow, which should've looked stupid on anyone except me, but on Sissily everything looked good. If she wasn't my best friend and if I had magic, I would've hexed her with warts. I hoped the girl knew how lucky she was that I loved her like a sister. What surprised me more was she loved me back the same, even though I was an asshole. At least most of the time.

"I've always told you fashion is a weapon if you learn how to use it. Did you believe me? Of course you didn't." My smirk earned me a twitch of her mouth. If anyone knew Sissily they'd know it for the huge win that was. She never smiled on a job.

"Danika is going to lose her shit." We both shivered at that.

As if saying the name conjured her, my grandmother's power preceded her presence, filling the warehouse with magic and saturating the air with the strong scent of ozone.

"Hazel Byrne." I flinched when my name echoed in the silent building, and Sissily copied me sympathetically. "Show your face this instant." My grandmother swooped in like a hungry vulture honing-in on a roadkill.

Me. I was the roadkill.

Thankfully, the lights came on inside the building, blinding me momentarily as thumps of many feet scattered throughout the warehouse. Our coven mates spread around the vast space like ants. I blinked like an idiot a few times until my vision cleared, and that was when I saw the look on her face. Cold, emerald eyes sharp enough to cut a diamond rolled over me from head to toe, assessing and judging while telling me she found me lacking in many ways. I gulped and tugged Sissily's jacket closer. Then Danika's unreadable gaze fell on Davon, who took a lesson from the Kishi demon and was starfishing it in the middle of the damn place. She stilled at the sight of a human cop and stabbed me with a glare afterwards.

"That was Sissily, not me." The words burst from me so fast I almost spit on my lower lip.

"Snitch," my best friend hissed, but her chin jutted out and she stepped closer to me.

"Every bitch for herself, remember?" I mumbled behind my hand when I raised it to wipe my mouth in case I was still drooling. Those Manhattans were buzzing in my head like a cloud of bees and making my tongue too thick for my mouth while I swayed where I stood. Oh boy was I screwed.

Sissily snorted but coughed to cover it up. Her reaction earned me a disapproving look from my grandmother, which I felt all the way to my soul. The woman saw everything no matter how hard I tried to hide it, and her hearing was better than a vampire's. I didn't have to guess because I *knew* she heard us.

I was the best fighter they had in our coven. Hand-to-hand or weapon combat, I could take them all down, and that included our high priest. But thanks to my lack of magic, I somehow always ended up looked down on, especially by Danika Byrne. Even when I did get the job done.

One demon stabbed in the throat with a designer boot, case and point.

"We will speak back at the coven." With flare, she spun on her heel, her long dress billowing behind her as she stormed out of the warehouse and left me grinding my teeth.

"Let's go." Linking her hand through mine, Sissily tugged me along with her because she probably assumed I would run. And honestly, I thought about it for like two point five seconds. It was pointless since everything I had was in the house I shared with my grandmother, but it sure was tempting. I wobble-limped alongside Sissily, glancing at my coven mates as they packed everything, including the Kishi demon I apprehended.

"She will chill out by the time we get back." My best friend gnawed on her lower lip, not believing her own assurances.

"I don't care." My shrug didn't fool her since I was patting my hair to smooth it and probably looked constipated just thinking about facing my grandmother behind closed doors.

Because Danika Byrnes never chilled. Like ever. My grandmother was born with a stick so far up her ass the goddess herself couldn't find it if she tried.

She was going to hand my ass to me, and I had no other choice but to take whatever she dished out. A sinking suspicion that it would involve cleaning churned in my stomach right beside the booze.

There was a first time for everything, though. She might've grown a heart in the last twelve hours. Or took it from some random jar and shoved it in her chest. My head tilted to the side, I contemplated it for a second.

One look at my grandmother's disappearing form, with

The High Priestess

those stiff shoulders and that head held high, killed that hope. There was no escaping a punishment.

With a groan, I followed my best friend into the belly of the beast.

The whole way back to the coven, I kept trying to picture my eyeballs floating in a jar on top of my grandmother's desk.

They were a nice shade of golden honey, if I did say so myself. I'd have them in a jar too if I didn't need them.

Resting Witch Face: Chapter Two

The Gatekeeper's coven was located dab smack in the middle of Cleveland, of all places. The temple walls stretched high toward the sky like the open mouths of baby birds waiting for a worm to fall into their gaping maws. A domed ceiling made of glass, to better see the full moon each month, covered almost half the block. Made out of black stone, the building looked menacing, and the three keys – a symbol representing Hecate- painted in blood red above the tall double doors of the entrance stood out stark against it. Since it was late at night, magical flames were shooting seven feet tall on each side of the stars leading to it, casting it in an eerie-hellish hue. No wonder humans gave us a wide berth.

Pausing at the bottom of the marble steps that would lead me inside, I glanced up and down the street. An urge to book it down the sidewalk and find a place to hide for a day or two was very tempting. However, with only one boot and still mostly drunk, there was no way I could outrun Sissily. She might sympathize with me, but she was a stickler for the rules, and she was smart enough not to want to anger Danika, unlike me. I had no doubt she'd tackle me and drag me kicking and screaming inside by the hair. She did that once in middle school when I didn't want to go back inside with her after lunch break. The humans mulling around would be no help, either. Ever since we came out of the closet, so to speak, they gawked like we were circus freaks but wouldn't come closer than a few feet, as if magic was contagious and they might get infected. I wish it was.

There were exceptions like Davon the cop, but those were few and far between. We were "the others," and unless they needed help, humans wanted nothing to do with us. At least there were no pitchforks or burnings at the stake involved, so not bad I guessed. That was why my coven was very strict. The government told us we were all good to live among humans as long as no problems came up by *any* supernatural being, not just us. So, the high priest and my grandmother—to be honest it was probably all her because the priest was practically a mute when around her—decided we would boss the supernatural world around. The magi police force was just a front for posturing. We were the ones that got down and dirty. And destroyed perfectly new pairs of designer boots in the process, I'd like to add.

Sissily took my elbow and waddled me up the steps when I took too long to move. Chewing on the inside of my mouth, I allowed my fear to choke me until I reached the double doors, and then I squared my shoulders. Whatever issues I had would be left at the door. No one needed to know my shit. It was none of their business, anyway.

The inside of the building was also painted black, with a hallway like one long intestine twisting around offices, ritual rooms, guest reception halls, and the library, of course. Our pride and joy, with knowledge gathered for generation after generation by magical families. It was the largest collection in the world, and the love of my grandmother's life. I personally used it to hide from idiots when they got annoying, or to pretend I was busy when we had a ritual scheduled. If I was busy, I couldn't participate and see all the pitying looks or sneers thrown my way.

"You ready?" Sissily mumbled under her breath and dragged me out of my spinning thoughts.

"No."

"Hazel."

"Why does everyone think saying my name will help anything?" I jerked my elbow out of her pinching hold and tugged hard on the borrowed jacket to straighten it. My balance went sideways, and I pitched forward, but she tugged me back before I face planted. "Let me tell you, it does nothing but piss me off and feed my anxiety. I know what my name is. I've had it my whole life, thank you very much."

"You're stalling."

"No." I gasped dramatically. "What in the world gave you that idea?" Sissily rolled her blue peepers at me. "I really don't want to go in. I might puke all over her desk."

"You're so stupid." She snickered and bumped my shoulder. For her sake, my lips pulled to the side in a pathetic attempt at a smile.

With a sigh, I continued my impersonation of Quasimodo hobbling down the hall on one high-heeled boot and one bare foot, darting glances at the candelabras lining the walls. Black pillar candles burned in clusters with blue flames, the magical fire standing straight without a crackle or a flicker. They always looked like a painting that gave off light to me, and it didn't matter how many times I saw them.

The High Priestess

"They are expecting you." We hadn't fully rounded the corner yet, but Mike made sure to shout it like he was playing bingo and just won. He leered at Sissily, but as soon as he met my glare, his head ducked down so fast he almost headbutted the desk.

"I see you didn't take your meds today, Mike?" I jabbed him conversationally, and Sissily snorted.

"What? Yes, I did." His face snapped up and reddened like a tomato. "Hey, I don't take medication."

I pursed my lips, eyeing him and pretending like I didn't believe him.

Something told me if I kept looking at him his head might explode. I was willing to test that theory, but I felt Danika's magic reaching, plus Sissily nudged me to get moving.

"Maybe you should." My suggestion to the creep in passing left him sneering. "Meds won't grow your brain, but it'll help with your complexion."

We left him stuttering and talking to himself about bitches and the goddess knew what other fairy tales he told himself. After he dared to treat my best friend like she was his personal punching bag while she dated him, I made it my business to mess him up every chance I had. I was pretty sure he cast a protection spell around himself specifically against me so I couldn't physically harm him. Good thing, too, because I didn't trust myself not to fillet him like a fish.

I flung the door open without a knock and hobble-hopped inside my grandmother's office with Sissily nipping on my heels. Stopping in my tracks, I took in the large, ornate-oak desk Danika Byrne sat ramrod straight behind. High Priest Shadowblood was behind her right shoulder, his face pinched so tight it looked like he was trying not to fart. His slicked dark hair, long, thin nose, and pointed chin brought the image of a crow perched on my grandmother's shoulder to my mind every time he did that, although I never dared mention it. But it wasn't those two that made me freeze with one foot in the air and one hand gripping the doorknob.

No, it was the third person in the room just to the left of Danika. In his late twenties to mid-thirties, he was a face I'd never seen before between these walls. His blond hair was shaved close to his skull on the sides, with the top left longer to drape over his forehead in a wave. Eyes the color of melted chocolate flicked my way when I opened the door, and they widened in interest—not enough to be obvious, but since I was staring at him like an idiot, I noticed. A square jaw and a nose with a slight bump at the bridge like it had been broken a time or two framed full lips more suitable to a woman than someone like him. Wide shoulders stretched his indigo button-down shirt, which was tucked into the waistband of dark slacks that emphasized his narrow waist and muscular body. I gawked for less than five seconds, but it was enough for one corner of his mouth to twitch. That little quirk snapped me out of my daze.

Spinning around, I bolted out of the office and plowed Sissily down. She would've fallen on her ass if I didn't catch her by the arm and drag her back out with me. The door closed behind us with a loud thump when I bodily carried her to the desk where Mike was still muttering curses at me.

"Give me your shoes." My best friend squeaked when I plopped her ass on the desk.

"What? Why?"

"Shoes woman. Now." My hand was wiggling in her face to show my urgency. "Questions later."

I yanked them off her feet myself because I had no time to explain why having shoes instead of one boot—regardless of how pretty said boot may look—was so important. Lifting her leg up pushed Sissily until she was leaning on her hands, and if I wasn't in a hurry I would've chortled at Mike's face. Poor schmuck almost swallowed his tongue when he received a face full of a ponytail, and his saucer-like eyes told me he didn't miss Sissily's boobs sticking up from her arched back. I even stabbed her foot in my one boot because I was a good friend like that, and then I was yanking her along with me to enter the office for the second time. She'd probably replace my shampoo with glue to pay me back for this, but I'd deal with it later.

When I stepped back inside the office, my grandmother arched an eyebrow not looking very pleased, which I ignored, of course. Being the nice little witch I was, I waited for Sissily to limp inside before I closed the door and guided her to the closest chair. Her blue eyes were spitting daggers at me the whole time. As Sissily dropped on the uncomfortable chair, I went as far as petting her head like a puppy that did potty, ignoring her glare the entire time. Then, I turned and beamed at everyone in the room, giving my grandmother a pointed look towards blondie that said help a girl out but I had a feeling my plea fell on deaf ears.

"Hazel, what happened tonight?" Danika Byrne got down to business, stapling her fingers under her chin and leaning her forearms heavily on the desk. If looks could kill, Sissily would be reading my obituary right now.

Smile frozen on my face to flash my pearly whites, I widened my eyes at her. "What?" My lips didn't move as I pushed the question through my teeth. My best friend groaned from the side.

"What in the goddess's name is wrong with you?" I swore lightning flashed in Danika's emerald eyes. "Are you hurt? Did the demon do anything to you?"

"We don't discuss coven business in front of strangers, Dani—I mean, Ma'am. Grandmother," I added that last bit lamely as an afterthought, and the thunderous expression twisting her features told me she didn't miss it.

"River Blackman is an apprentice of our high priest, Hazel." She looked down her nose at me like I was supposed to be psychic and guess who was who around here without introduction. "There are no strangers."

Wait, what?

"You can have your shoes back." With a groan, I turned to Sissily and started tugging the shoes off my feet. I shoved them in her face, and she recoiled as if I'd thrown snakes at her.

"I don't want them." She attempted to slap my hands away with a mortified look on her face, but I was very persistent when I needed to be.

"Well, you're having them." I jabbed them at her again. "Give me my boot."

"What in the world is going on?" We all ignored the high priest when he mumbled at no one in particular, sounding perplexed.

"You are aware that you are nuts, right?" Sissily muttered under her breath, but she tugged her shoes on, and I yanked the one boot over my foot.

"Of course. I'm an asshole, Sissily, but I'm not stupid." She blinked at my incredulous tone, but I was already turning toward the rest of the people in the room.

A muscle twitched under my grandmother's eye.

"When the call came for the demon, everyone that answered was at least twenty minutes away. Everyone in this room knows they are sneaky and fast." I figured I'd get it over with. "I was closest to the demon, so I answered the call and made sure he didn't escape. Long story short, he is in our hands and the warehouse ransacked ..." Danika's scowl was a creature all on its own. "I'm sure you don't want to hear my internal debate about sacrificing my new boots so he didn't get away, Grandmother."

Grating on my nerves was the fact that River's eyes were dancing with suppressed humor. *Laugh it up, asshole, because I'll make you cry soon enough.* I wasn't sure he read the message I shot his way through my narrowed gaze, but he couldn't say he wasn't warned. Being a dud was a sure thing to get you bullied in a coven full of powerful witches, so instead of dealing with that, I became a master at cracking their noses with my fist. The blondie wouldn't know what hit him.

"I do want to hear every detail there is. Starting with what possessed you to go there in the first place. Fighting a demon without magic is unacceptable." If she noticed my flinch, she didn't show it. "He could've killed the last of the Byrne line, you insolent girl."

"How's this for a recap, Danika?" I snarled. The gasp from Shadowblood sounded scandalized when I slapped both hands on her desk and leaned forward so we were at eye level. "I can kick any demon's ass, including every idiot you have inside this coven, in six-inch heels, without breaking a sweat, and with my arms tied behind my back. I showed up at the warehouse, cracked the demon's head on the concrete like a melon, then I stabbed him with my new boot. Which you owe me a new pair, plus an iPhone, just so you know. Then the rest of you waltzed into posture with your magic and clean up the place. That good enough of an explanation for you?"

"How dare you speak like that?" High Priest Shadowblood stuttered, his neck elongating as he tucked his chin in. "You are not a savage, young lady."

"Aren't I, though?"

"Show respect to your grandmother," he snapped.

"You got one thing right, pops." My empty stare flicked his way, and he took an involuntary step back. *If they don't string me from the roof tonight, I'm honestly never drinking again.* "*My* grandmother, and I'm doing exactly what she taught me. To quote her, 'you treat people the way they treat you.' So, I will talk to her however damn well I please. In this case, I'm showing her the same respect she gave me." I believe Shadowblood was about to have an aneurism.

"Hazel," Danika leaned back in her chair on a sigh, all fight draining out of her. "I wasn't trying to insult you because you have no magic."

For an old witch, barely any lines were visible on her beautiful face. She might be a stick-up-the-ass nag, but no one could dispute the fact she still turned heads. Midnight blue hair spilled around her face like a waterfall, bringing attention to her alabaster skin and piercing emerald eyes. Tall for a woman, she was curvy where it counted, but most admirable of all was her presence. When Danika Byrne walked into a room, you knew it even if your back was turned.

"No, you were complimenting me on a job well done." With one last stare at Shadowblood, I pushed off the desk. "If we are done here, I need a shower. I can smell the Kishi demon on my skin."

"I need you to promise me—"

"I will not step foot anywhere where your precious witches with magic need to go." My smile could cut glass when I looked at her over my shoulder. "I'll just stand back and look pretty."

"You are not replaceable, Miss Byrne—" Shadowblood started, but I cut him off.

"No, I'm to be kept as a broodmare, High Priest Shadowblood. I'm aware." That got the reaction I expected from my grandmother.

"For the next week, you will be cleaning the library, Hazel," Danika snapped and stood to her full height, which was a couple of inches higher than mine. She did it on purpose so I had to look up at her. *Nice power play, Grandma.* "And the ritual room, too, until I say that you are done. Am I clear?"

"Crystal." I dared a glance at River, but with his hands clasped at the small of his back, he was frowning at his boots. *Welcome to the Gatekeeper's Coven, blondie, this is how we treat family.* The guy hasn't done anything to me, but just seeing him standing behind that desk with Danika and Shadowblood put him in my shit bucket, too.

"Let's go," I called out to my best friend, who was in the office for moral support more than anything else.

We almost made it out the door. Almost.

"Sissily, you'll join Hazel in her tasks." My grandmother was already back in her chair and had turned to say something to River Blackman, a blunt dismissal of us if ever I saw one.

We spilled out of the office without another word. "Why do I pay every time you get into trouble, little jerk?"

"Because you are the only one that can call me that and live, big jerk." I threaded my arm through hers, leaning against her for support.

"True." She sighed and placed her head on my shoulder. "On a good note, not even you can get in trouble inside a library."

Lesson 2: *never tempt fate.*

That bitch bit.

Resting Witch Face: Chapter Three

"Hazel?"

Sissily's tone was low when she hissed my name, but in the silence of the library, it boomed like a gun going off next to my ear. My head jerked up for no reason at all since I knew she'd be coming to join me. The back of my skull connected with the thick wooden shelf above me with a dull heavy thud, which made dark roses bloom at the corners of my eyes as I crawled backward, extracting myself from my hidey hole. I had no doubt my best friend had a perfect view of my ass sticking up in the air while I wiggled my way out, but my glare made sure any comment she had stayed behind her closed mouth.

Her lips stayed pressed closed for exactly thirty seconds. Tops.

"I still don't understand why you had to take my shoes," Sissily grumbled under her breath, still stuck on the same thing two days later as she handed me a stack of ancient texts we had to catalogue. Courtesy of the Kishi demon I nailed with my poor ankle boot.

The High Priestess

"That should be your answer." Her elbow connected with my side, forcing me to grunt. Exasperated, I huffed, shaking the books in my hands at her face. "You can't understand why you would need to leave a good first impression because you have magic, woman. That's all a guy in our world needs to feel and he gets the googly eyes. I, on the other hand, don't have magic. Apart from the respect I receive around here …"

"That's not respect, Hazel. They're afraid of you. There is a difference," she told me so calmly you'd think she just gave me a compliment.

"That's beside the point. As I was saying, I only have the respect, so I have to make a good impression with my sense of style, too." We both knew I was talking smack. If I stopped doing that, I would have to curl up in a ball and start rocking back and forth.

"I still don't get the shoes."

"Hecate help me, would you stop with the damned shoes? I didn't want to limp on one boot like a dumbass in front of a hottie, okay? How was I to know blondie was one of Grandmother's pawns?" Admitting my vanity was never easy, although she knew me better than I knew myself.

"He is easy on the eyes, I'll give you that." A smile ghosted her mouth, and she bumped me with her shoulder while tucking a loose strand of hair behind her ear.

"Great. Have at it because he is all yours. In the meantime, grab that stack of books over there." Pointing my chin at the pile ready to tip over, I pushed the last book in my hands on the shelf between two others.

In a normal life, when someone told you that you'd be cleaning a library, you'd expect rows of books lining the walls and pretty tables with single little lamps where people could read in peace and quiet. Since nothing was as it should be in this place, half of the vast room was packed with jars full of floating eyeballs, teeth, fingers, or other body parts I tried very hard not to pay too close attention to. A shiver raked my spine, and my friend noticed.

"Ignore those, I'll fix them up." Sissily allowed me to keep my dignity because we both knew I'd end up begging her to do it so I didn't have to touch them. "I honestly don't know why you insist that everyone thinks you are this mean little shit when you have a heart of gold." She shuffled back to me with an armful of tomes, not missing my grimace. "You can say whatever you want, but I know you."

"I should kill you so you keep my secret, then." I snatched the books, turning my back so she didn't see the tears that prickled the back of my eyes.

"Do try, I'm begging you," my friend purred, cocking her hip.

Sissily was the strongest witch in our coven after Danika and Shadowblood. She had every right to be cocky, and for the life of me, up to this day, I couldn't tell why she chose me to be best friends with. By doing that, she made sure her name was whispered behind our backs by all the petty witches in our community, too. A fact that rubbed me wrong on so many levels and made me bare my teeth at everyone, while she couldn't care less about the gossip mill. Regardless of what she said, it was her with the heart of gold, taking strays—or duds as it was in my case—under her protection. Coven mates tried using their magic against me at the beginning, knowing I couldn't fight back the same way, until she unleashed ropes of fire and sent a few of them to the infirmary with third-degree burns. Danika was ready to peel the skin off her bones until she walked in and saw us with arms wrapped around each other, jutting our chins at her in defiance. After a long, loaded look, my

The High Priestess

grandmother's mouth twitched at the edges and she walked away without a word. We were four at the time, and since that day, we'd been glued at the hip. Unfortunately for my friend, that meant she got in a lot of trouble because of me. I had no magic, but I had fists.

"Do I look dumb to you?" I pointed at myself. "I didn't think so."

Sissily giggled and walked to the floor-to-ceiling shelves full of jars across from where I was standing. "How much longer do you think she will hold us here?" In jeans, a t-shirt, and with her hair in a ponytail, she looked comfy, unlike me in my skirt and blouse.

"I don't know," I answered honestly with a sigh. "If I kept my mouth shut, we may have gone without punishment, but I just couldn't let that go. I swear sometimes I think Danika says things on purpose because she knows I'll react. If I didn't know better, I'd say she rubs salt in an open wound when she needs both of us out of her way."

"What do you mean?" Sissily twisted toward me, hugging a jar full of imp fingers to her chest.

I sawed my teeth over my lower lip, contemplating if I should voice my thoughts or keep my mouth shut. When her blue eyes narrowed on me, I knew I better speak up or she'd never let it go. My best friend was as stubborn as a mule.

"She knows that not having magic is a sore subject for me." Eyes darting around to make sure no one was around, I took a couple of steps closer to her, keeping my tone low. "It's a sore subject for her, too, since I've heard her raging about idiots and how they didn't value their lives because they treated me like I was nothing. So why else would she slap my lack of magic in my face unless she wanted me punished and out of her way?"

I could almost hear the gears turning in Sissily's head. The corners of her mouth slanted slightly down, and the edges of her eyes narrowed. She had her thinking face on while her eyes searched mine.

"Every time I'm punished, you are in the same boat, too …" I trailed off.

"In the last seven to eight months, more so than ever." Sissily nodded, the jars completely forgotten.

"Well, now that you mention it, yeah." Frowning, I ignored the unease swirling inside me. Witches came to their full potential of power at the age of twenty-three, which for both of us was a few years ago. My best friend and I had our birthdays three days apart, and we were both twenty-six now, so that couldn't be the reason for Danika tucking us away more often than usual. "I can't think of a reason—"

"I can." Plonking the jar with a loud thump, Sissily snatched my hand and dragged me deeper between the rows of books. "About nine months ago, the other covens called a meeting in Atlanta. Do you remember?" She waited for my head to dip in confirmation before continuing. "According to Mike—"

"You still talk to that douchebag?" My mouth closed shut with a snap when she shot me a glare.

"The other covens pressured Danika to reassess the contributions of her coven because it's not fair"—She used air quotes and twisted her mouth— "for most of the Gatekeeper's Coven to be in power. Apparently, they had witches in their ranks, which would be a better fit for enforcers. I think the new guy is here for that reason, by the way."

"And I jumped in to apprehend a Kishi demon with no magic at all." With a groan, I buried my face in both hands, ignoring the comment about River.

The High Priestess

"Yeah." Her nails dug into my forearm where she was still holding onto me. "So, if what you have noticed is true, I will bet my magic it has something to do with that."

"There you are, Hazel." The words died on my tongue, and I spun around to face the witch smirking at us from the other end of the shelves. I wanted to tell Sissily what I said was only a suspicion gnawing at me and not facts, but it'd have to wait.

"Is there a reason you are breathing the same air as me?" I asked Sasha Airborne, nemesis number one from our coven. Sissily clutching my arm made it look like she was holding me so I didn't jump the witch, which worked in my favor.

She took a step back before catching herself.

"The crescent moon chamber needs to be cleaned for the midnight ritual." Her drawled words made me grind my teeth, and Sissily clamped her fingers harder on my forearm. "The High Priest Shadowblood said you need to do it stat. So chop-chop, get to it."

"Hazel ..." Sissily hissed, but I shook her off and was already striding to Sasha.

The witch didn't have time to bolt before I stood in front of her and grabbed a fistful of her shirt, twisting it in my grip to bring us nose to nose. She could've been beautiful with her flame-red hair and sky-blue eyes, if she wasn't a snake.

"Last time I checked, Shadowblood is perfectly capable of speaking for himself. Why are you here?" My crazy eyes reflected back at me in her wide-eyed gaze. This close, I'd knock her ass out before she had time to call on her magic, and we both knew it.

When the warmth of magical flames washed over my back, I knew Sasha was debating whether or not to take a chance, especially since Sissily stood behind me giving her a light show with her fire magic. Venom burned in Sasha's eyes, and she answered through clenched teeth.

"I told him I was coming this way and I'd pass the message along."

"You didn't learn your lesson last time you decided to pick on someone stronger than you?" Her skin paled, telling me she remembered the time when she decided it'd be fun to corner me with her friends and they cut my face and arms using air magic. They had me pinned like a bug on the wall and chortled like it was all fun and games. For them, it might've been. I had a different opinion on the matter.

That memory was burned in my brain along with the crippling pain of feeling my skin splitting open and the grating sound of their laughter while I begged them to stop. It was one of the few times Sissily was not with me, and they took full advantage of that. We were eleven. I couldn't remember much of how things played out after that, just that I came out of the daze on my knees with Sasha and her friends beaten to a bloody pulp around me. Something dark and hungry swirled in my chest when I thought about it, whispering in the back of my mind that I should make her suffer.

"Everything okay here, ladies?"

I released Sasha at the sound of the smooth baritone that washed over us like a balm. She stumbled away from me, throwing a glare over her shoulder as she darted out of the library and shouldered out right past River Blackman. Before I could grab her, Sissily bolted too, turning my way only after she was behind River, grinning like a fool and giving me a thumbs up.

Like a somersault, my stomach dipped when his raspy

chuckle filled the library and he stepped inside. My shoulders hunched as if preparing me to run for the door, which was stupid on so many levels, but he closed the heavy door with a thud that held some finality to it.

Goosebumps popped up over my arms when I met his brown eyes and saw the intensity there.

"I don't believe we were properly introduced." Blondie swaggered closer until I could feel the warmth of his nearness through my clothes. "I'm River."

"Hecate cursed me." As soon as I realized I spoke out loud, my gaze snapped up to meet his.

"I'd say it made you quirky and very intriguing, Miss Byrne." A smile ghosted over his full mouth before it turned into a panty-melting grin. "I won't say cursed, unless that's what you make of it, of course."

Why did he have to be buddies with Shadowblood and my grandmother? Why?

Grab your copy...
vinci-books.com/restingwitch

About the Author

Maya Daniels, USA Today Bestselling and multi-award-winning supernatural suspense author, is a fun-loving woman with many talents.

She traveled the world, gaining life experiences that helped her career as an investigative journalist, as well as her storytelling. Maya writes compelling tales of magic, mythical creatures, loyalty, and life-changing friendships with snarky female characters—much like herself.

Her travels have taken her to Europe, Africa, Asia, Australia, and America. Born with her feet in motion, she currently resides in Ohio, spinning her next epic story that you will not want to put down.

Her biggest 'sins' are her love of chocolate and coffee—through an IV drip! One to never sit still, Maya practices Reiki healing, different types of martial arts, reads about the arcane, talks to furry creatures more than humans, picks up a sledgehammer for home improvement, and travels with her fated mate, seeking her own adventures.